CRUMBLED!

LISA HARKRADER

**YELLOW
JACKET**

YELLOW JACKET
an imprint of Little Bee Books

251 Park Avenue South, New York, NY 10010
Copyright © 2019 by Lisa Harkrader
All rights reserved, including the right of reproduction in whole or in part in any form.
Yellow Jacket and associated colophon are trademarks of Little Bee Books.
Interior designed by Tim Palin Creative
Manufactured in China TPL 0819
First Edition
10 9 8 7 6 5 4 3 2 1
Library of Congress Cataloging-in-Publication Data
Names: Harkrader, Lisa, author.
Title: Crumbled! / by Lisa Harkrader.
Description: First edition. | New York, NY: Yellow Jacket, 2019.
Series: [Misadventures of Nobbin Swill; 1] | Summary: When Nobbin Swill, a royal dung farmer, ventures to the castle, he is drawn into hapless Prince Charming's quest to solve the case of the woodcutter's missing children, Hansel and Gretel. | Identifiers: LCCN 2019018447
Subjects: | CYAC: Fairy tales. | Characters in literature—Fiction. | Missing children—Fiction. | Princes—Fiction. | Mystery and detective stories. | Humorous stories. | BISAC: JUVENILE FICTION / Fairy Tales & Folklore / General. | JUVENILE FICTION / Humorous Stories. | JUVENILE FICTION / Mysteries & Detective Stories. | Classification: LCC PZ8.H22 (ebook) LCC PZ8.H22 Cru 2019 (print) | DDC [Fic]—dc23
LC record available at https://lccn.loc.gov/2019018447
ISBN 978-1-4998-0971-8 (hc) / 978-1-4998-0972-5 (ebook)
yellowjacketreads.com

For my sweet elves: Ashley, Austin, and Larry

Contents

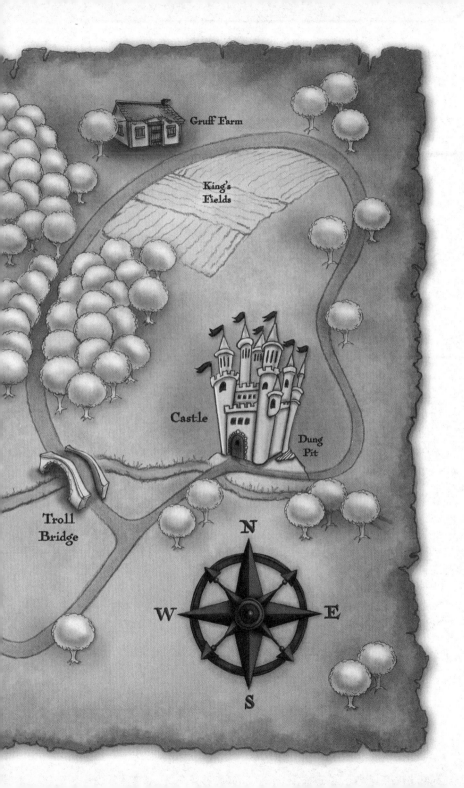

1

A Rustle in the Night

Once upon a time, I was a dung farmer. I was a sorely miserable dung farmer from a proud family of dung farmers. After tonight, I would never farm dung again.

It was going to come as a big surprise to my father.

It was midnight. The castle towered above us, black against the moon. The stench of the dung pit rose up through the dark. My heart thumped against the rustling bit of paper tucked into my tunic.

I gave one last pull, and the cart creaked to a stop. My father and brothers piled off, shovels and buckets clanking.

"Lout!" my father bellowed at my oldest brother. "Put your back into it. The dung won't shovel itself."

"Snout!" he barked at my second-oldest brother. "Pay attention to what you're doing. The king won't put up with shoddy work, and neither will I."

"Gerald!" he boomed at my third-oldest brother, who would've been the youngest if not for me. "Mind how you dump the buckets. I'll not have you sully the good name of Swill."

For that was our name: Swill.

Lout, Snout, and Gerald Swill.

And me, Nobbin.

Plus our father.

Lout and Snout slogged down into the dung pit. Lout shoveled dung into a bucket. Snout heaved the bucket up to Gerald. Gerald dumped the dung into the cart, dropped the bucket back down to Snout, and the whole thing started again.

My job was to level it out. I snatched up my rake and climbed onto the cart.

Not everyone had a dung pit. Village folk had chamber pots. We Swills had an outhouse, tumbledown as it was. And at the castle up on the hill, the king had a dung pit, with a garderobe high in the tower above it.

The garderobe was a little room off the king's very bedchamber, so folks said. It held a kingly seat with a hole in it. The hole led to the dung chute, which ran the length of the tower and emptied into the dung pit below—the very pit my brothers were now shoveling dung out of.

Folks also said the king used the garderobe to store his finery. His cloaks, his robes, his furs and velvets. The stench was supposed to ward off fleas. That part, I could believe. We Swills were crusty and cruddy and ragged and rank. We were not, however, flea-bitten.

As I balanced on the edge of the cart, raking dung, I gazed down at our village of Twigg.

Not a creature was stirring, save a family of ducks skimming across the mill pond. Six yellow ducklings glided after their mother in a neat row. Paddling away at the end was their enormous and fuzzy gray brother, like a stump of wood bobbing behind sweet daisies.

The surrounding houses of Twigg were dark, buckled up for the night. The tinker's. The tailor's. The shoemaker's shop. The odd, boot-shaped house with all the children. The woodcutter's cottage tucked snug against the forest, a tendril of smoke curling up from its chimney.

I leaned against the rake. Maybe soon, I would be like them. Maybe soon, I would sleep cozy in my bed until morning. Maybe soon, I—

"Nobbin!" my father's voice pounded the night air. "Quit your lollygagging and get back to work!"

Work. Yes.

"Can—can I talk to you about that?" I managed to say.

"Talk?" My father cocked a woolly eyebrow.

I climbed down from the cart. I reached into my tunic.

A week ago, I'd found a button in the dung. The next night, I'd found another. Two matching buttons! It was a rare find. I'd cleaned them up and traded them to the village scribe for a handful of torn and tattered papers. I kept them close to my chest, safe from my brothers. On one of the scraps, I'd sketched my idea.

Now, I smoothed the wrinkled edges of the page, took a breath, and held it up.

2

A Glimmer in the Dung

$\mathfrak{T}$he paper quivered in my hands. Moonlight fell across the lines of my drawing.

My father gave it a suspicious look.

I swallowed the dry lump in my throat. "It's a dung-scooping machine," I said. "The buckets are attached to a rope. They scoop the dung, dump it in the cart, then drop down into the pit for more." I moved a finger over the lines as I explained. "All we have to do is crank the handle."

My father snatched the paper from my hands. He held it close to his face.

For one hopeful moment, I thought he was studying it. I thought he was considering its usefulness. For that tiny bit of a moment, I thought—

"Crank?" my father's voice thundered. "Swills don't crank. We shovel. It was good enough for my father and my father's father and *his* father before him. It's good enough for you."

He crumpled the paper in his fist and chucked it into the cart. I watched it turn brown and disappear into the dung.

"Quit dreaming up fool contraptions"—he shoved the rake at my chest—"and get to work."

I stared down at my boots. "Yes, sir," I whispered.

My father stalked off. I climbed onto the cart and peered inside. My drawing had vanished somewhere beneath the muck.

But as I teetered there, on the edge of the cart, a glint of moonlight caught my eye—the light was glimmering off something in the dung.

It was probably only a shard of pottery.

Or a bent nail.

But I'd never seen pots or nails catch the moonlight with such gumption.

What if it were another button?

Or a thimble?

Or no—a shoe buckle.

With a good scrubbing and a spit polish on the cleanest edge of my tunic, a buckle would fetch me a coin from the shoemaker.

Two if it weren't bent.

Three if the shoemaker's wife weren't around to chase me off before the smell of me scared away paying customers.

I glanced over my shoulder. My brothers were busy shoveling dung. My father was busy bellowing at them to shovel faster. Nobody was busy watching the cart—

—except me.

I plunged my hand into the dung and quickly plucked the shiny bit out.

3

A Poke in the Rib

I didn't dare look at it. Not there. Not with my brothers lurking. I slid the shiny bit into my tunic and snatched up the rake.

As I smoothed the dung, I tried to make out what the shiny bit might be.

It was too big for a button. Too round for a shoe buckle. Too heavy for a thimble, and not jagged enough for a shard of pottery. I shifted in my tunic. Whatever it was, it was making a sharp dent in my ribs.

At long last, the cart was full, the dung pit empty. We sloshed out to His Majesty's fields to dump the king's dung.

When we finished, I picked up the handles of the empty cart once more. My father gave it a shove to get me going. Lout, Snout, and Gerald heaved themselves aboard.

My father marched ahead.

"I'll not wait," he roared back at us. "I'm tired to my very bones. If you want to see your beds tonight, quit dillydallying and start moving."

He disappeared down the road.

We rumbled along behind, down the hill toward Twigg.

To get there, we had to cross the bridge.

And the troll who lived beneath.

I'd never seen the troll. But I'd heard stories, mostly from Lout and Snout.

"The troll likes meat," Lout had told me.

"Raw meat," said Snout.

"And bones—the crunchier, the better," said Lout.

I was skinny, so I was probably pretty crunchy. A lot crunchier than my brothers.

The bridge loomed ahead. My steps slowed. My stomach squeezed into my throat.

Behind me, Lout snickered. "What's wrong, Nobbin? Scared?"

"The troll," said Gerald. "I bet he's scared of the troll."

"You're a genius," said Snout.

"Really?" said Gerald.

"No," said Snout.

"You probably heard about the goats," said Lout.

"Oh, yeah," said Snout. "I did hear something about some goats."

"What happened?" said Gerald. "What happened to the goats?"

"It's a sad story," said Lout. "Three goats left the Gruff farm, headed for greener pastures. But first, they had to cross the bridge."

"The bridge?" said Gerald. "*This* bridge? Did they see him? Did they see the troll?"

"No one knows," said Lout. "They started across . . . and vanished."

"Vanished?" said Gerald.

"Disappeared," said Snout.

"Where'd they go?" Gerald's voice was a squeak.

"No one knows," Lout said again. "When Farmer Gruff went looking for them, the only thing he found was the little brass bell from the smallest goat lying in the middle of the bridge. That's all that was left."

Gerald yelped.

Snout snickered.

"You're making that up," I said.

"You hope," said Lout.

I did hope.

I stared at the bridge.

Each night, I had two choices: Slow down and try to sneak across without waking the troll. Or speed up and sprint across before his gnarled hand could reach up and snatch me.

Each night, I made the same choice.

I gripped the cart handles. I took one step, then another, and another, till I was running, pulling the cart—and my brothers—at full speed.

Ba-DUMP! Ba-DUMP!

We bumped onto the bridge.

Thu-RUMP! Thu-RUMP!

My heart hammered in my chest.

Four steps, and I would be across.

Three. Only two to go.

Two.

The cart bounced. A blob of dung splatted onto the cobblestone in front of me. I stepped onto it and—

Sloosh.

My foot shot out from under me.

Bam!

The cart handles banged against the ground.

Bump!

Thump!

WHUMP!!!

My brothers tumbled from the cart.

"OOOF!"

Somebody's boot caught me square in the back. I skidded across the bridge, slammed belly first into the bridge rail, and tipped over.

I clung to the stone, half dangling over the edge.

That's when I saw him.

I didn't know he was there at first. It was pure blackness under the bridge.

Then he opened an eye. Just one at first. It was bulging and yellow and shot through with veins.

And huge.

I'd never seen an eye so big. It stared up from the darkness. Stared at me with its big, yellow, red-veined awfulness.

My fingers slipped.

This was it. This was the moment I would be eaten by the troll.

My fingers slid.

The moment I would vanish forever, like the goats.

My fingers trembled.

I would never find out what was poking my ribs.

My fingernails scraped across stone.

For that's all they would find of me—one shiny bit, smaller than the smallest goat's brass bell. A shiny bit burped up by the troll as he finished off the last delectable morsel of my skinny, crunchy bones.

My grip tore loose.

I toppled over the edge.

4

A Hand in the Dark

PLOSH!

I plunged into the icy water.

"ULLLP!"

The cold knocked the air from my lungs.

I began to sink into the dark depths, thrashing for something—anything—to pull myself up. My hands latched onto a rock. A solid, dependable rock . . .

. . . slimed with moss.

My hands slipped. The rushing water wrenched me loose.

As I swirled downstream, something splashed into the water beside me.

It was a hand.

It was huge.

It was powerful.

It was . . . soft.

Like a big leather cushion.

The cushion caught me. It wrapped nearly all of me up in its enormous palm. It scooped me from the water.

And suddenly, I was face-to-face—

—with the troll. With his eyes, both of them open this time, huge, yellow, and bloodshot.

He looked at me.

I looked at him.

He lifted me above his head.

The better to slide me into his mouth, I thought.

This was it.

He lifted me higher.

I squeezed my eyes shut.

He pushed me. Not hard. Just enough to set me onto the bridge. Enough to stand me upright on wobbly legs.

Then he just let go.

I opened my eyes.

He nodded his big, shaggy head. Just once. Then he melted into the darkness.

I stood on the bridge, shivering and gasping for breath. Water dripped from my tunic.

"Do you see him?" Snout's raspy whisper echoed across the bridge.

My brothers were bunched together on the other side, their backs to me. They peered down at the water.

"He probably got sucked downstream," said Lout.

"Who's going to pull the cart now?" said Gerald.

"*I'm* not," said Snout.

"Me neither," said Gerald.

"Well, one of you has to," said Lout, "because *I'm* not going to do it!"

I coughed up a lungful of water.

My brothers spun around.

"There he is!"

"We thought you were a goner."

"Like the goats."

"Did you see him? Did you see the troll?"

I nodded.

"Was he huge?"

"Was he awful?"

"How did you fight him off?"

I tried to shake my head. But all I could do was cough up water. I pressed a cold-numbed hand against my ribs. By some miracle, the poky bit was still there.

I dripped back to the cart and hoisted the handles.

5

A Thief on the Roof

Ⓣhe sun was just peeking over the trees when we finally trundled up to Swill Cottage.

"Cottage" was a bit optimistic. "Hovel" was more like it. Or, if we're being honest, "Rickety-pile-of-sticks-that-would've-tumbled-over-if-not-for-the-heaps-of-rubbish-stacked-against-the-walls."

It hunkered at the very edge of the village—far from the other houses, far enough for no one to catch a whiff, so far that the other villagers could pretend it wasn't part of the village at all.

My father was already home. His snores shook the whole hovel. My brothers burst into the house. Soon, their snores joined his, like the blare of four rusty trumpets. Old MacDonald's pigs at the feed trough gave out a sweeter sound.

And mostly likely a sweeter scent.

A stick of a tree grew in the dirt patch beside our door. I grabbed hold, shinnied up, and swung myself onto the tattered thatch of our roof.

From there, I could see past our tumbledown dirt plot to the village and beyond. I could see the butcher and the baker, the cobbler and the candlestick maker. I could hear the peddler jangling through Twigg and, in the distance, the farmer's rooster crowing in the dell. I could see the woodcutter's cottage tucked against the trees, where the village stopped and the forest began. It could have been a twin to our cottage, two bookends on either side of Twigg.

If I were a strapping brisket of a man like my
father, maybe I'd march through the village with my
head high and my chest out. Maybe I'd laugh when the
other villagers held their noses. Maybe I'd brag about
a dung-farming job well done.

I sighed.

No, probably not.

I listened for a moment to make sure my brothers
were still snoring their off-key snores, then slid my
hand into my tunic and pulled out the poky bit.

It felt heavy in my hand. Heavy and round and
bumpy. I rubbed it against my tunic to wipe off the
last bit of dung, held it up in the gray morning light—
—and caught my breath.

It wasn't a button.

Or a shoe buckle.

Or a bent nail, dented thimble, or broken shard of
pottery.

It was—

I blinked.

—a ring.

A gold ring. At least,
I thought it was. I'd never
seen gold before.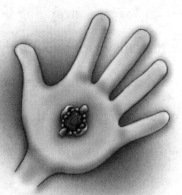

I barely saw it now. The ring was covered in
jewels—green, blue, and, the largest, a deep red with
the shape of a lion carved upon its face. It glittered so
brightly, it nearly blinded me.

A ring like this would fetch more than a coin. It
would fetch a handful of coins. A cart full. A ring like
this would fetch—

I stopped. I could scarcely breathe at the thought.

A ring like this would fetch a life free from dung.

I closed my fist around it. With a ring like this, I
could go anywhere. I could be anyone.

I could smell . . . like a real person. I'd never smelt
like a person before.

As I sat there, marveling at the sweet-smelling possibilities, the town crier's trumpet blared through the village.

My mind startled back to the tattered rooftop. I frowned. I'd never known the crier to cry his cries at this early hour of the morning.

"Hear ye! Hear ye!" cried the crier. "The king's royal signet ring—"

Ring? I blinked.

"—has been stolen by a treacherous, traitorous, lily-livered thief."

6

A Hoard in the Hovel

Thief?

As the last blast of the crier's trumpet faded into the early morning mist, village doors creaked open. Townsfolk, still in their bedclothes, peeked out, yawning and rubbing their eyes.

I hunkered behind our crumbling chimney. I kept my fist closed even tighter around the shiny bit.

I wasn't a thief.

I was . . . a finder.

The king lost a ring.

I found a ring.

And who said it was the same ring anyway? Just because the one I found was shiny and gold and covered in jewels, worth a king's fortune, and fished from the king's dung pit.

As I gripped my fist against my chest, the trumpet blared once more.

"All the king's horses and all the king's men," cried the crier, "will search the village—"

A chill crept up my spine.

"—until they find the king's royal ring," cried the crier.

I froze. If the king's men came to the village, they'd start at the first place they arrived: Swill Cottage.

I wasn't worried about the ring. I'd once hidden a whole roast beef from my brothers. I could hide a ring from the king's men.

But what about our dented teakettle? And our
wobbly stool? And our three bent forks and two
tarnished spoons and Snout's mismatched boots and
the frayed rope that held Gerald's pants up? We'd
fished them from the dung, too, along with nearly
everything else we owned.

I couldn't hide it all.

I leaned against the chimney, trying to think about
what to do.

Swills weren't thieves. We found things other people had tossed aside.

But we found them in the king's own dung. To the king, that might be as good as stealing. And the king's men would discover it all.

They would arrest us. They would throw us in the dungeon.

The king would never let a Swill shovel his dung again.

I wouldn't mind that so much. A dungeon might be a big improvement over the dung pit.

But what about my father? Shoveling dung was good enough for his father and his father's father and *his* father before him. If he didn't have dung, my father would have . . . nothing.

I opened my fist—

—and stared.

Not at the ring. At my hand.

It was clean, so *clean* it was almost pink. Even under the fingernails.

And my *clothes*. I glanced down. They were nearly dry now. And they weren't dung-crusted. They were clean, too. Raggedy, but clean.

And red.

My tunic was red. I had no idea. I'd gotten it from Gerald once he outgrew it. He'd gotten it from Snout, who'd gotten it from Lout. Who knows where Lout got it? But all this time, under all that dung, it was red.

I sniffed my sleeve. It smelled like . . . sleeve, I think. I wasn't sure what a sleeve was supposed to smell like. The stream I'd fallen into had washed away every bit of dung from my body, even the stench.

I slid down the spindly tree and cranked a bucket of water from the well. I stared into the water. A strange boy stared back. I squeaked and jumped away. The bucket splashed into the well.

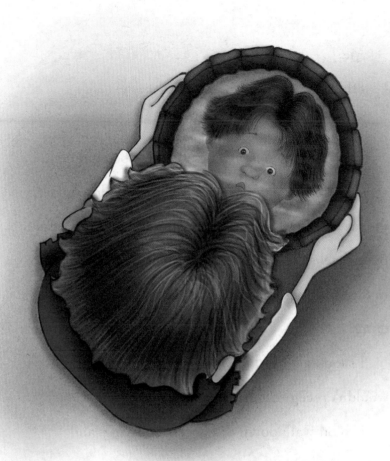

I gave myself a good shake, then cranked the

bucket up once more. I sneaked a peek into the water a

second time.

The boy peeking back . . . was me.

I stared at him.

Me.

Him.

Me.

I was used to everything about me being dung-smeared. And dung-crusted. And dung-colored. But the face staring back had a clean pink nose. And clean pink cheeks. The hair, a light ginger color, fluttered in the morning breeze, free from the crunchy layer of dung.

I shook my head in wonder. My own father wouldn't recognize me.

I could walk down the streets of Twigg, and villagers wouldn't cross to the other side.

I could walk into the shoe shop, and the shoemaker's wife wouldn't chase me out.

I could walk straight up to the king himself, and he would never know I was a Swill.

I stopped.

He would never know I was a Swill.

I dropped the bucket back into the well.

I slid the ring back into the folds of my tunic.

I set off for the castle.

7

A Swill at the Gate

The gatehouse door stretched above me. A heavy iron knocker hung above my head.

Hope bubbled in my chest. I hadn't passed the king's men marching down the hill as I'd been scurrying up it. If I could return the king's ring quickly enough, perhaps I could stop them from marching to the village at all.

Normally, the castle gate stood open during the day. Village folk needed to get in and out to go about their business. Bring wood. Deliver eggs. Clean the chimneys. Sneak a ring back in that should never have gotten out in the first place.

But today, it stood bolted shut.

I leaped and batted the knocker. A loud *CLANK* echoed throughout the gatehouse.

I leaped and clanked once more.

A small hatch was cut high into the thick planks of the door. Suddenly, the hatch squeaked open. The gatehouse guard peered out, his face round and red and bristly, topped by a lumpy leather cap.

The guard squinted to one side, then the other. He poked a sausage finger against the bridge of his nose.

"Um . . . down here," I said.

He looked down. His squint fixed on me. For one terrifying moment, I was afraid he would recognize me. Our dung cart rumbled past the gatehouse each night, to and from the dung pit. I was sure he'd know me for the Swill I was.

But he just squinted and grunted and said, "State your business."

I took a breath. "I'm here to see the king," I said, trying to keep my voice from wobbling.

The guard shook his head. "No can do. Nobody's to come in or out of the castle. Strict orders. Not till His Majesty gets his ring back."

He started to slam the hatch.

"Wait!" I said. "That's why I'm here. I've got—"

The hatch squeaked back open.

The guard squinted and poked at the bridge of his nose. "You've got what?"

"I've got—"

I swallowed. My heart hammered against the ring tucked into my tunic.

"I've got a talent for finding things," I said.

"Things?" The guard gave me a sideways squint. "What kind of things?"

"Things like"—I swallowed again, more confident this time—"eyeglasses."

"Eyeglasses?" His squint became extra squinty. "Who said anything about eyeglasses? Nobody here has eyeglasses."

"No," I said. "But if someone did, and if he misplaced them, he may have pushed them up on his head and forgotten them. He might find them under his cap."

The guard gave me a suspicious squint. He lifted his lumpy cap with one hand, then pushed his other hand underneath. He felt around and finally pulled out a pair of small, round spectacles.

"Well, would you look at that!" He slid on his glasses right above his nose and patted his cap back in place.

The hatch door slammed shut.

The gatehouse door rumbled open.

8

A Guard with a Wish

The guard's name was Ulff.

When he'd first opened the hatch, he'd looked
huge.

When he'd squinted down at me, he'd seemed
fearsome.

But now, as my eyes adjusted to the dim light
inside the gatehouse, I saw he wasn't much taller than
I was. Every bit of him was round and red and bristly,

like his face. But he'd had to stand on a stool to see out of the gate.

"What's your name?" he asked me.

I hesitated, but only for a moment. Around Twigg, I was called One of Those Swills. Or That Dung Boy— the Scrawny One. Or worse (usually by my brothers).

I knew my first name wouldn't give me away.

"Nobbin," I said.

"Nobbin what?"

"Just . . . Nobbin."

Ulff nodded as if I'd said something wise.

"You're not from around here, are you, Nobbin? Know how I know?" He tapped a stubby finger against his head. "It's all up here. Once I've seen a face, I don't forget it. And I've never seen yours."

I nodded as if that were true. And, in fact, it was. He'd seen the crusty layer of dung I'd worn before this day, but he'd never seen the face beneath.

He looked me up and down. He straightened my belt. He rubbed a spot on my sleeve. He stood back and studied me. I looked pretty much the same as I did when I walked in, but Ulff gave a sharp nod.

"Fit to see the king," he said.

Ulff stashed his footstool behind a suit of armor. He tucked his eyeglasses up his sleeve. He led me from the gatehouse and across the courtyard toward the castle proper, scuttling quickly over the cobblestones so that I nearly had to run to keep up.

As I squelched along in still-damp boots, a shiver washed over me. I wasn't sure if it was the dank chill of the courtyard or the sudden realization of what I was doing. I'd gained entry to the castle grounds. But I hadn't thought much beyond that. I hadn't thought what would happen once I'd gotten inside. I couldn't just walk up to His Majesty the King and say, "Here's your ring. You must've dropped it down the privy while you were doing your business."

"So," Ulff said to me over his shoulder, "how'd you know I lost my glasses? Most folks don't even know I wear them." He lowered his voice. "I like to keep that kind of thing to myself."

"Uh—well," I said, thinking fast. "You can't be good at finding things unless you know what's lost."

It must've sounded good. Ulff nodded again.

"You're a clever lad, young Nobbin. If you find the king's ring, I can only imagine how grateful His Majesty will be. Grateful enough to bestow a generous reward to the finder, I'd wager."

Reward? I nearly stopped in my tracks. I hadn't thought of a reward. Keeping the Swills out of the king's dungeon seemed reward enough.

Still, if the king were that grateful, and if he were so inclined . . .

"And to think, *I'm* the one what found you." Ulff shook his head in wonder. "I found the lad who might probably find"—his voice slowed, and so did his step— "the king's own ring."

He stood there for a moment, eyes wide.

He turned to me. "I'm a gatehouse guard, Nobbin.

And if you don't mind me saying, I'm a good gatehouse guard. But no one pays me much attention. You may not have noticed, but I'm on the short side of tall. People look over my head."

I nodded. No one paid me much attention, either.

But I was glad of it. I'd learned early on that less attention meant more freedom. Those times when no one was looking were the times I could do what I needed to do. They were the precious gaps between what the world had in mind for me, and what I had in mind for myself.

By this time, we'd reached the castle. Ulff gave an absent *thump thu-thump thump* on the great wooden door.

"I wouldn't mind if someone noticed me," he said. "If they noticed my skill, my loyalty. I wouldn't mind if someone thought I was worthy enough to take my place among the ranks of—"

The door yawned open, and Ulff's voice caught in his throat. Before us stood a line of soldiers, their shields and surcoats gleaming.

"—the king's men," whispered Ulff.

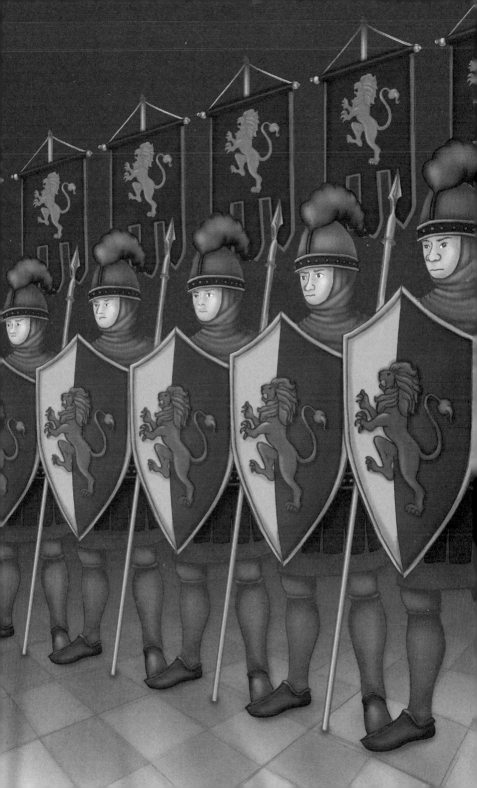

9

A Prince in a Pickle

"O*h!*" I took a step back.

Ulff nodded. His eyes glistened. He gazed up at the king's men, who stood in tight formation in the main hall.

"They're still here," I said, mostly to myself.

Ulff nodded again. "But not for long. We'd best hurry. The king'll be that much more impressed if you find his ring before he sends his men off to ransack the village."

He led me around the wall of soldiers and through an archway.

Pig's pantaloons! I nearly went blind on the spot. We stood in a large, round room. Light shimmered from every surface. From the marble floors. From the golden chandeliers. From the silk of the ladies' gowns.

A crowd of stately people ringed the room. Lords and ladies of the court, I guessed.

Ulff tipped his head. At the far end, wide marble steps led to a throne. And upon the throne—

—sat the king.

I scarcely breathed. I'd spent my life under the king's latrine. I'd shoveled his dung. I'd fished his bent and broken castoffs out from the pit.

But I'd never seen the king himself. Not proper. Not more than a wave of his fur-draped arm through the window of his royal carriage.

And now here he sat, a mere cart's length away from where I stood. His hands clenched the intricately carved armrests of his throne. His forehead was creased into a knot of worry.

I shivered again. At first, I thought it was from seeing the king up close for the first time. Then I realized I was well and truly chilled. For all its gilt and finery, the king's throne room was bone cold. My breath puffed out in white wisps before my face.

"I'm old enough." A young man in a suit of armor stood before the king, a plumed helmet tucked smartly under his arm. "*I* should lead the men."

Ulff elbowed me. "The king's eldest." He tipped his head toward the young man.

"Prince Charming?" I asked.

Ulff nodded.

"I'll have your ring back to you anon, father," the prince was saying. "You know my skills."

"Yes." The king pinched his knotted brow. "I do."

"Your *Majesty*." A man I'd not noticed before oozed from the shadow of the throne.

I choked back a gasp.

The man gave the king a pained smile, his thin mustache stretched tight above his lip. "I'm as eager as anyone for young Charming to finally prove himself."

"And that"—Ulff's nostrils curled as if he'd just caught a whiff of dung—"is Sir Roderick."

I nodded. I hadn't known his name. But I'd seen him before. And he may have seen me, though I doubt he much noticed.

He'd come to the dung pit a fortnight ago. The king usually sent a messenger with payment for my father's dung farming, but this time, this man—this Sir Roderick—had come. He stayed as distant from all of us as he possibly could, stretching his long arm out as far as it would reach to drop the bag of coins into my father's hand, then yanking his arm back quickly. As he turned to leave, he chanced a small sniff and a quick glance at the dung pit, and gave a nod of satisfaction. Then he'd disappeared back into the castle.

Now he waved a finely gloved hand at the prince. "But Your Majesty only just allowed him to take over the daily operations of the castle not two weeks ago. The bitter cold in this very throne room shows how well he's done with that."

"I'm as perplexed as you by the cold, good Sir Roderick," said Charming. "I've been trying to get to the bottom—"

"And now squirrels," said Sir Roderick. "In the pantry."

Charming frowned. "Squirrels? This is the first I've heard of it."

"Yes, well." Sir Roderick ran a finger over his mustache. "It only just happened. Cook heard their scratching and skittering. Fortunately, I was there to bolt the pantry door." He turned to the king. "Your Highness, the prince means well, I'm sure. But we're talking about Your Majesty's royal signet ring."

Ring. Yes.

I slid my hand into my tunic and gripped the ring in my fist. I'd scooped it from the dung right under my brothers' noses. Surely, I could get it back to the king with no one the wiser.

I turned a full circle, studying the room. I scarcely noticed the thin runner of a carpet beneath my feet—

—until I tripped over the turned-up edge of it and nearly tumbled headlong into a nearby lady's skirts.

The ring shot from my grasp, sailed high over the throne room, and landed beneath the edge of a bit of drapery with a soft *thunk*.

10

A Trick of the Carpet

Ulff caught my flailing arm and pulled me upright.

"Best watch the rugs around here," he said in a low voice. "It wouldn't do for you to go tail over teakettle in front of the king."

I nodded. But I wasn't listening. I was desperately peering around the skirts of the ladies and through the legs of the lords, trying to catch sight of the ring.

"I have prepared a lifetime for this very moment,"

Charming was saying. "Allow me to use the royal virtues—honor, loyalty, gallantry, valor—"

Sir Roderick gave a low snort. "The village tailor is more valiant," he muttered.

"—to find the king's royal ring and restore it to its proper place." Charming pressed a palm to the breastplate of his armor and gazed into the distance above the heads of the lords and ladies. "On the king's royal finger."

He placed his helmet on his head, squared his shoulders, and, still gazing off into the distance, took a princely step—

—over the edge of the marble stairs. Legs flew, arms flailed, and plume bobbed as he bumped and thrashed down the steps. He landed with a deafening *clank* at the bottom.

The lords and ladies gasped.

Then sighed in relief as the prince rattled back up to his feet.

"Nothing like a brisk jaunt down a staircase to stimulate mind and body." He straightened his plume. "And now, to find the ring!"

He took another princely step. His toe caught on the upturned edge of the carpet, and he pitched forward.

"OOOF!"

He landed with a *clunk* on his breastplate and skidded across the floor, his armor skimming over the polished marble like a skate on ice.

Lords leaped to one side, ladies to the other. The prince shot between them, headlong toward a marble pillar, only saving himself when his arm hooked some heavy drapery. He spun into a tangle of folds.

The lords and ladies stood silent. Or mostly silent. Here and there a twitter of laughter escaped the crowd. The king groaned and pressed a hand across his eyes. Sir Roderick arched an eyebrow, the corners of his mouth turning up in a small, satisfied smile.

"Speaking of tail over teakettle," Ulff whispered.

I nodded. But in that moment, I saw opportunity. Opportunity in the form of a glimmer, a glint of gold and gemstones glistening beneath the edge of the drapery, mere inches from Charming's armored hand.

I grabbed Ulff's arm.

"He found it!" I whispered. I pointed to that glimmering glint of gems. "He found the ring!"

Ulff frowned. "Who found the ring?" His voice echoed through the throne room.

"He found the ring?" the lords and ladies murmured.

The king sat up. Sir Roderick narrowed his eyes.

Prince Charming fought his way free of the drapery.

He blinked. He plucked the ring off the floor and held it high.

"I found the ring!" he said.

Ulff scratched his head. "Well. Would you look at that."

"Yes," Sir Roderick fairly growled beside the king. "Would you look at that indeed."

"Huzzah!" cried the lords and ladies.

Sir Roderick glared at the prince, then at Ulff.

Then his gaze settled on me.

A chill trickled down my spine, and not from the cold of the room. Sir Roderick's black eyes bored through me. Bored through my clean red tunic. Bored through to my very core, till I was sure he could see the Swill inside.

I took a step back, then one more. He couldn't know who I was. He couldn't. He'd never even glanced in my direction when he'd been at the dung pit. Still, I needed to get to the archway, and to the door beyond, and back to the hovel, where a proper Swill belonged.

Before I could make another step, the crowd parted, and the town crier panted into the throne room. He bent over for a moment, hands on his knees. Out of breath, no doubt, from crying all over the village. After a few gasps, a cough, and a rasping wheeze, he straightened and lifted his trumpet to his mouth.

The king waved him off with a flick of his hand. "No need for pomp and blast. Just say what you came to say."

The crier nodded, strode to the throne, and snapped his heels together.

"Hear ye, hear ye," he cried.

With a rustle, he unfurled a parchment scroll and began to read.

"Two children from the village," he cried, "have gone missing!"

11

A Lad Under Wing

Two children from the village. My heart thumped.

I was a child. I was only one child, not two. And I wasn't missing. Not exactly. I knew where I was. But my father didn't. Nor my brothers.

My *brothers*!

My heart thumped again.

Lout, Snout, and Gerald weren't anybody's idea of children. Not of the young and innocent variety, at least. And I'd gladly do without the torment of their

71

company for a time. Not to mention they hadn't seemed all that concerned when they thought *I* might be gone forever, eaten by a troll.

Still, I wouldn't want two of them to go missing.

Leastways, not for long.

"From the village?" The king leaned forward, his face creased with worry. "Which children?"

I held my breath.

The crier cleared his throat. "A girl—"

A girl. I let out my breath. My brothers were likely still snoring away in the hovel, not a care to be had in their thick skulls.

"—named Gretel," said the crier.

Gretel? Now my heart well and truly stopped.

"And a boy named—" The crier ran his finger down the scroll.

Not Hansel, I thought. *Don't say Hansel.*

"Hansel," said the crier. "A boy named Hansel. Gretel's younger brother."

A murmur rippled through the court.

"The woodcutter's children?" the king asked,
sitting back in his throne.

I swallowed.

Hansel and Gretel.

I knew them.

Not properly. A dung farmer's son never knows
anyone properly.

But I felt a kinship toward them.

And not just because our two cottages sat like
bookends on opposite ends of the village. In truth, our
lives were like opposite sides of a coin.

Their father worked for the king, same as mine.
He kept the wood cut and stacked for the castle.
The difference being that no one minded the smell
of woodsmoke from a warm fire, or if the man who
brought the logs for it smelled smoky. I couldn't say the
same for dung.

And they'd started their lives without a mother,
same as me. But another woman had come along to
marry their father and care for his children. Not many
women would willingly take on a house full of Swills.

"Fear not, Father," said Charming with a flourish
of his hand. "I shall lead the search to find yon
youngsters."

The king pinched the knot between his eyes.

"Your *Majesty*. I hardly think . . ." Sir Roderick stopped. A dark look flickered across his face. He seemed to roll a new thought over in his mind. His lips curled into a smile. "I suppose it *would* give the prince a chance to show his true valor."

The king sighed. "Yes, I'm afraid it would. Very well," he told the prince. "Go. Talk to the woodcutter. Find out what happened."

Charming gave a low bow, the plume of his helmet skimming the marble floor. "Your trust is not misplaced, sire. I shall find the lost children, just as I found the missing ring."

"Yes." The king tapped a finger against his lips. "Just as you found the ring."

Now it was the king who seemed to be rolling a new thought.

"You there." He waved his finger in my direction.

I glanced about, hoping to glimpse which lord or lady he was pointing to.

There was no one.

I swallowed. "Me, sire?"

"What is your name?"
said the king.

"I—"

"This is Nobbin,
Your Majesty." Ulff
clasped my arm.
"And I'm Ulff. Your
gatehouse guard. I'm the one what found him." He thrust
me toward the king and stood beside me, his cap crumpled
in his bristly red hands.

"Nobbin." The king studied me thoughtfully. "Have
we met?"

"No," I said. It was not a lie.

"He's not from around here," said Ulff.

The king nodded. "You seem to have your wits
about you, Nobbin. It was you who noticed Charming
had found my ring even before the prince did himself.

Accompany him to the village."

I nearly choked. "To the—?"

"Quite right, Father." Charming placed an armored hand on my shoulder. "I shall take young Nobbin under my wing. Teach the lad a thing or two."

"Your *Majesty*." Sir Roderick gave me a thin, hard smile. "This young urchin—"

"—will assist in the search," responded the king.

Sir Roderick narrowed his eyes. His glare bored through me. His mouth twisted this way and that.

Then it curled into a thin, hard smile once more.

"Yes," he said. "This urchin will do nicely."

"And me, Your Majesty?" Ulff clutched his cap, his eyes hopeful. "The one what found him?"

"Very well." The king waved a hand. "You may accompany the prince as well."

And just like that, I was Prince Charming's assistant.

And Ulff, it seemed, was mine.

12

A Journey to Twigg

Clunk.

Clank.

"Hunf."

The royal groom hoisted Prince Charming onto his faithful steed, Darnell.

The prince held a small mitten. Only one.

"A damsel left this behind last night at the ball," he explained. "Just before midnight, as it happens. You'd be surprised what turns up in the castle after a party. I couldn't find her to give it back, but I thought it might bring us luck."

He tucked the mitten into one of his shiny armor gauntlets.

Then he spurred Darnell to action.

"To the village!" he cried. "Make haste!"

Darnell slowly turned and ambled down the hill toward Twigg. Ulff and I scuffed along behind on foot.

And I had to hand it to Charming. He clattered a bit in his armor, but he cut a fine figure. His plume bobbed. His steed clopped. The morning sun glinted off his helmet. As long as he wasn't trying to do anything, he looked every inch the valiant prince.

I felt a prickling on my back, as if someone were watching. I glanced back. At first, I thought I saw movement on the battlement atop the tower. But when I looked again, it was gone.

I shook my head. It was only my own fear creeping up my spine.

Ulff tucked in beside me. Our boots crunched over the rough pebbles.

"This is our chance." He kept his voice low, but his round body quivered with excitement. "If you do a good job, Nobbin, you could become the prince's assistant permanent-like."

I allowed myself to imagine this. Of me, living in the castle, trailing after the prince, walking light in boots that weren't weighed down by an inch of dung.

"And me," Ulff continued. "I've finally come to the attention of the king himself. If I do a good job, who knows what might become of me?"

He took a moment to breathe in the possibilities.

"And I have you to thank for it." He turned to me, his eyes wide. "If you hadn't shown up like you did, why, I'd still be back at the castle, guarding the gate."

I swallowed. If he knew who I truly was, I doubt he'd thank me so.

We wound our way down the hill, through a thicket of trees, and around a bend. Ahead lay Swill Cottage. My father and brothers were still asleep. Even at this distance, their off-key snores rocked the roadway.

I had a quick thought of trying to join them. Of slipping through the trees and back to the hovel when Charming, Ulff, and Darnell were looking elsewhere. My father and brothers would never know I was gone. With a smear of dung on my face and tunic, Ulff and the prince would never know I was the lad at the castle. They'd likely not come close enough to look anyway.

I glanced at Ulff, his face so so eager, the very bristles on his cheeks quivered with hope. I swallowed. He was counting on me. He shouldn't be. But he was.

I couldn't abandon him.

As we passed the hovel, I stayed on the far side of Darnell. I couldn't take a chance one of my brothers might stumble out to use the privy and spy me strolling along the roadway with His Royal Highness.

Soon, we were winding our way through Twigg. The streets were empty, the shops shut tight.

The prince reined Darnell to a stop. "I always thought this a lively village," he said. "Where can everyone be? Nobbin, make a note of it. It may yet be a clue."

I rustled in my tunic and pulled out another of the tattered scraps I'd gotten from the scribe. It was still damp, but I found a dry edge and wrote *Village—quiet.*

The prince spurred Darnell on. We clopped on till
we reached the end of the high street and turned toward
the woodcutter's cottage.

"Well," said Ulff. "Would you look at that."

The entire village, it seemed, had gathered there.
The miller and his daughter. The shoemaker and his
wife. The goose girl, the huntsman, the dwarfs from
the forest. The widow from the end of the lane kept a
sharp eye on her big-footed daughters—and an even
sharper eye on their scullery maid. A red-cloaked girl
clutched a basket of goodies to her chest, while the odd
little peddler lurked at the edge of the crowd. They all
clustered outside the woodcutter's cottage, speaking
in hushed tones. Mr. and Mrs. Woodcutter huddled
together before the front door.

"Whoa!" called the prince.

Darnell clopped to a halt.

Everyone turned.

"It's the prince!" someone cried.

The men bowed. The ladies curtsied. The children hid behind their parents' legs, eyes wide, gaping at Prince Charming.

The Woodcutters hurried to greet him.

"Your Highness!" said the woodcutter's wife.

The woodcutter removed his cap and twisted it in his hands. He kept his head down, barely meeting the prince's eye.

"After all that's happened," he said, "we weren't sure you'd come."

13

A Letter from the King

"Of course I would come," said Charming.

He moved to dismount, but his foot caught in the stirrup. He thrashed and flailed, struggling to wrench it free.

Ulff leaned toward him. "Maybe you should stay mounted. Seeing's how you're His Royal Highness and all."

"Excellent thought," said the prince, struggling to get fully upright. "But I'm here to help. I must be among the people."

He gave a kick, and his foot popped free. He swung his leg over Darnell and—

Clank.

Clatter.

"Hunf!"

—toppled to the ground, his other foot still caught in its stirrup. Darnell wheezed. Ulff and I scrambled to free the prince.

"Thank you, my good men." Charming sprung to his feet, righted his breastplate, and turned to the Woodcutters. "Your children," he said. "They're missing."

Mrs. Woodcutter nodded. Her eyes filled with tears.

"I tucked them in last night," she said. "I gave them warm milk. I read them a story. I left them safe and snug and—" A sob escaped her throat.

A sob nearly escaped mine.

Swill Cottage had but two beds, one as lumpy as the other. My father took the first. My brothers slept three across in the other. I curled up lengthways at their feet, their smelly toes jammed in my face. Snout twitched. Gerald itched. Lout flopped one way, then the other. Most days, I ended up on the floor with one of Gerald's boots as a pillow.

"This morning, I called them for breakfast," Mrs. Woodcutter was saying. "But they were gone."

A murmur burbled through the crowd.

I frowned. It was before breakfast when I'd climbed onto our tattered roof. I often spied Hansel and Gretel from my perch up there. I would hear the bang of their cottage door and see them bound out. I'd watch them chase each other around the garden and hug their father as he set off to chop wood.

But had I seen them that morning? I closed my eyes and tried to think back.

I'd seen smoke curling from the bake shop chimney.

I'd caught the scent of baking bread. I'd heard a door, yes. But it didn't bang. It creaked. I'd heard the rooster crow and had made out the rattling jangle of the peddler making his way up the high street.

I opened my eyes.

I spotted the peddler then, lurking behind the miller's daughter. What had he seen that morning?

"Quite the sticky wicket," Charming was saying. He tapped an armored finger against his lips. "How to proceed, how to proceed . . ."

"Maybe get a description of the children?" I whispered.

"Yes!" Charming turned to the Woodcutters. "What do your children look like?" To me he said, "Transcribe this, young Nobbin."

I knew full well what Hansel and Gretel looked like, but I thought a likeness might be handy as we searched for them. As Mrs. Woodcutter described her children, I sketched them in my notes.

Gretel

Hansel

While I sketched, I glanced up at Mrs. Woodcutter, then back down at my page. That's how I happened to notice a small trace of something on the Woodcutters' doorstep. Something small and dark and crumbly. Not dirt. I knew dirt well enough. This was a bit of—I sniffed—a bit of—

"Aunt Betty's bloomers!"

I looked up, startled.

Charming was pacing. "This is a travesty," he said. "Two children—vanished! Plucked from under the very nose of their mother."

"Stepmother," called a voice from the crowd.

Charming stopped. "Stepmother? I've heard something about stepmothers. What was it?" He tapped his finger again, trying to recall. "Oh, yes! They're wicked."

The villagers gasped.

"Wicked?" Mrs. Woodcutter's face crumpled.

The young woman with the dwarfs nodded. "Indeed. My stepmother's a nightmare."

"But I love those children as if they were my own," said Mrs. Woodcutter.

"Maybe," said the shoemaker's wife. "But I heard her say that the kids eat too much."

"*Sweets*," said Mrs. Woodcutter. "They eat too many *sweets*. I wanted them to—"

"And the woodcutter did just lose his job," said the miller. "Maybe they couldn't afford to feed them anymore."

The crowd murmured.

"Lost his job?" The prince furrowed his brow. "That can't be true." He turned to the woodcutter. "You're the *royal* woodcutter, are you not? As was your father and his father and his father before him. You bring wood for the castle's fires."

The woodcutter dropped his head. "Not anymore. Not since the king's letter arrived."

Mrs. Woodcutter sniffed. "It seems someone new is overseeing the castle, someone who thinks the woodcutter's services are no longer needed."

Charming frowned. "But the new person is me. And I would never think such a thing. Are you sure the letter was from my father?"

The woodcutter nodded. "Stamped with His Majesty's own seal."

I blinked. The king's own seal, stamped by the king's own ring—the very ring I'd found in the dung. He must have written it before the ring went missing.

"When did it arrive?" I said without thinking.

The crowd turned. They seemed to notice me for the first time. They narrowed their eyes. They elbowed each other.

They recognized me.

How could they not? They'd seen me often enough, skulking through alleyways, ducking the innkeeper's broom, pressing my face to the bakery window. I'd lived in the village all my life. I was a fool to think the villagers wouldn't know me.

Then I heard their whispers.

"Who *is* that?"

"And who does he think he is, interrupting the prince that way?"

"Must not be from around here."

"*I've* certainly never seen him."

"Nor I."

I blinked. They *didn't* know me.

I probably should've felt hurt. Instead, I felt . . . free. I was no longer One of Those Swills. Or That Dung Boy—the Scrawny One. Or worse.

I was just . . .

. . . me.

"Excellent question from my noble assistant," said the prince.

"*Assistant.*" Whispers rippled through the crowd. The villagers looked at me. With respect, I think. I wasn't sure. I'd never seen respect before. Not up close, anyway.

I swallowed. "So when did the letter arrive?" I asked again, a little louder.

"Yesterday," said the woodcutter.

"Yesterday." Charming clasped his chin.

Yesterday. So, the ring must have landed in the dung pit not long before I found it.

I waited for Charming to say something more, but he was still lost in thought.

"Maybe we should see this letter," I said.

"Yes!" The prince straightened. "We should see it now, shouldn't we?"

The woodcutter nodded and scuttered into his cottage.

He returned a few moments later. His hands were empty, his face pale.

"The letter," he said. "It's gone."

14

A Trail of Pebbles

"Gone?" Charming stared at the woodcutter. "Sow's spectacles! First the ring, then the children, and now the king's letter. I don't know what to say."

"Maybe you should ask if anything else is missing," I said.

The prince turned to the Woodcutters. "Has anything else gone missing?"

"Missing?" Mrs. Woodcutter shot a quick look at her husband, then shook her head. "No, I wouldn't

say so. I mean, there's nothing else"—she swallowed—
"missing."

"That's something to be grateful for, at least," said
the prince.

He seemed to believe her.

I wasn't so sure. I didn't think Mrs. Woodcutter
would harm Hansel and Gretel. But I'd kept plenty
of secrets in my life. I could tell when someone wasn't
telling the truth—or at least, not telling the whole truth.

I scribbled in my notes *Woodcutter's wife—hiding*
something.

Village-quiet
Woodcutter's wife—
hiding something

97

"Begging your pardon, Your Highness," said Ulff. "But wherever those children are, I'm sure they're scared. Probably hungry. Maybe we should look for them."

"Good point." The prince turned first one direction, then the other. "But where to start."

I chewed my lip. I'd seen Hansel and Gretel tagging along after their father when he went to cut wood. And I'd seen where they went to play.

"We should start with the forest," I whispered.

"The forest?" Ulff's eyes grew wide.

The huntsman stepped forward. "Just last week, I saw Mrs. Woodcutter take the children into the forest." He tipped his head toward the towering trees. "She came back. But the children did not."

The villagers gasped.

"The children were clever enough to leave a trail of pebbles," said the huntsman. "They managed to find their own way home."

"*I* left the pebbles," said Mrs. Woodcutter. "The children kept venturing farther and farther into the woods. I warned them not to. But they wouldn't listen. I taught them to leave a trail so they wouldn't get lost."

The dwarfs nodded.

"It's easy to get turned around out there," said one.

"Interesting." Charming narrowed his eyes. "The children often go into the forest. They know to leave a trail of pebbles." He looked up. "And did you find any pebbles this morning?"

The woodcutter shook his head.

"Ah!" The prince clanked his hands together. "That's excellent news."

"It is?" The Woodcutters looked hopeful.

"Most certainly," said the prince. "The children clearly didn't venture into the woods, then. There's no trail."

"Oh, I wouldn't say that." The peddler ambled out of the crowd, all pointy elbows and knees, the pots and forks in his coat jangling with each step. He gave the prince a low bow. "Rumpelstiltskin at your service." He straightened. "I saw a trail this morning when I was making my, er, rounds."

I blinked. I *knew* the peddler must have seen something.

"A trail of pebbles?" asked Charming.

"No," said Mr. Stiltskin. "A trail of crumbs."

15

A Trail of Crumbs

"Crumbs?" Mrs. Woodcutter's voice quivered. "Surely, you're mistaken."

"Surely, I'm not," replied Stiltskin.

Crumbs? That was it! I'd seen *crumbs*, too. I darted a quick glance at the Woodcutters' doorstep. But Mrs. Woodcutter's boot-clad feet now stood firmly on the precise spot where I'd spied the crumbling bit of something only moments before.

I looked at Mrs. Woodcutter.

She did not look back. And she did not move her feet.

"Crumbs." Charming chewed his lip.

"Should we ask where he found them?" I whispered.

"Quite so." Charming turned to the peddler. "Exactly where did you spot these alleged crumbs?"

"Where indeed? Let me think." Stiltskin tapped a finger against his lips. "It was a busy morning. Busy, *busy* morning. Here and there. To and fro. Hither and yon. Where *did* I see those crumbs?" He clucked his tongue. "A pity I have no gold. My thoughts seem to think themselves more clearly when I've a bit of gold to clutch in my palm."

"Gold?" The prince frowned.

Ulff leaned toward him. "The peddler wants payment."

The prince stared at him. "To find missing children? The scoundrel!"

Ulff nodded grimly.

"Ah, yes. Well . . ." The prince turned to Stiltskin. "We're out of luck on that count, I'm afraid. I've brought no coins on this journey."

"That *is* bad luck," agreed Stiltskin. "In that case, I suppose . . ." He paused, as if mulling over this unfortunate bit of news, then cut a sly glance at Charming. ". . . a ring might do."

"I've no ring, either," said the prince. "Alas."

"A pendant, then."

"Afraid not."

"A brooch?"

"None."

"A trinket, a bauble, a bead?"

The prince shook his head.

"I suppose a crown is out of the question?"

"Entirely," said Charming.

Stiltskin let out an exasperated breath. "Well then, what *do* you have?"

"Very little, I confess," said the prince. "Sir

Roderick keeps it locked up tight, especially now, considering the recent incident with my father's signet."

"Yes. A pity." Stiltskin's gaze darted this way and that, then locked on the edge of the mitten that was about to fall out of the prince's gauntlet.

The prince followed his look. "Oh, no. You shan't have the mitten." He tucked it firmly back inside. "It's meant to bring us luck."

"And has it?" asked the peddler.

"Not yet," admitted the prince. "But one never knows when it may kick in."

"Well, then." Stiltskin glanced at the helmet tucked under the prince's arm. A smile twitched the corners of his mouth. "Perhaps Your Highness could part with . . . a plume."

"A plume?" Charming pulled his helmet protectively against his breastplate. "Not *this* plume, surely."

"A royal plume would fetch a bit of gold in the

marketplace, no doubt. Or a few sheaves of straw."
Stiltskin shrugged. "One's as good as the other to me."

"But—" Charming swallowed. "But I can't surrender
my plume. It's my *plume*. As Sir Roderick says, the
feather makes the man."

"Actually." I cleared my throat. "I'd say the man
makes the feather."

Charming stared at me. "The man . . . makes the
feather?" He tumbled this about in his thoughts. He
looked from the plume to Stiltskin and back again. "I do
believe you're right, Nobbin."

He plucked the feather from his helmet.

"Apologies, dear plume," he told it. "If the man does
indeed make the feather, I fear what you are to become."
He handed the plume to the peddler. "Pray now, lead us
to these crumbs."

Stiltskin tucked the plume in his belt.

"Ah, yes." He pressed his fingertips to his forehead.
"It's all coming back to me."

He started around the cottage, and we followed. The villagers crowded in behind. Stiltskin stopped at a path that led through an opening in the trees.

"There." He pointed a knobbly finger. "That's where I saw them. A trail of crumbs from the Woodcutters' cottage leading into the forest."

We stared at the path.

It was empty of any crumbs.

"Devil's dishwater!" said the prince. "First a ring rustler, then a kidnapper, then a letter snatcher—"

"Then a feather swindler," said Ulff.

"—then a feather swindler," agreed Charming, "and now a crumb thief. Where will it end?"

"Woodland creatures do get hungry," said one of the dwarfs.

"Birds could've eaten them," said another.

"Or squirrels."

"Or wolves."

"Wolves?" Mrs. Woodcutter let out a cry.

The villagers twittered in fright. They began backing away.

Somewhere in the woods, a twig snapped.

Leaves rustled.

Screeeek. Screeeek.

Ulff clutched my arm. "What was that?"

"Naught but a friendly tree frog," said Charming. He gave Ulff an encouraging pat on the back. "Now, about these crumbs—" He turned to Rumpelstiltskin.

But the peddler had vanished—along with the rest of the villagers.

Only the Woodcutters remained.

"*Hrmph!* That's Twigg folk for you," muttered Ulff. "Quick to poke their noses in when it's none of their business. But the minute things get tricky—*pffft*. They're gone."

"I could show you where yonder path leads," said the woodcutter. "But Your Highness won't like it. It's—it's where the witch lives."

"Witch?" Ulff gulped. "The horrible woman who lures children into her house and—"

Mrs. Woodcutter sobbed. "I made the children promise they would never go near her cottage!"

She sagged against Mr. Woodcutter, who wrapped his arm around her.

Charming put a hand on the woodcutter's shoulder. "You should stay. Someone needs to be here to make warm milk when the little ones come home. My men and I can find the way. Our spirit will not be daunted by witches, nor wolves. Is that not true, men?"

Darnell's eyes grew wide.

Ulff swallowed. "Not daunted," he said. "Maybe a little terrified."

Charming took no notice. He slid his plumeless helmet back atop his head and took a firm grasp of Darnell's reins.

"To the woods!" He marched into the trees.

After a snort, a stomp, a shake of his head, and a

few tugs on his reins from the prince, Darnell followed.

I stood for a moment, looking after them. The prince didn't always know the right thing to do. He hardly ever knew the right question to ask. He almost never took a step without toppling onto his backside.

But he took the step anyway.

I didn't care what Sir Roderick said about him. Prince Charming had valor.

Ulff looked at me, eyes wide. "To the woods?"

I sucked in a breath. My heart pounded.

Not because I was scared.

I mean, I *was* scared. Plenty scared. I could barely feel my legs, I was that scared.

But my heart pounded because I was excited. I was eager. I was *ready*.

My whole life, I'd never been good at anything. I was a terrible dung farmer. I was a disappointing son. I *was* decent at outsmarting my brothers. I had to be.

But questioning witnesses, tracking down clues— *this* I was good at. *This* I could do. The prince had called my ideas excellent. Excellent! Nobody thought my ideas excellent before.

I scarcely dared think it, for Hansel and Gretel were still missing, but I believe I was enjoying myself.

I took a deep breath. I straightened my tunic. I looked Ulff square in the eye.

"To the woods," I told him.

16

A Walk in the Woods

We picked our way around gnarled roots and ancient trees, starting at every squawk and rustle.

As we climbed a low hill and rounded a bend, the birds around us suddenly startled from the trees in a fury of beating wings.

We stopped short. The forest was dead quiet.

And then, from somewhere behind us, a tinny *ping* echoed through the trees.

"What was that?" whispered Ulff.

"Sounded like a clink," I said.

"Or a clang," said the prince.

"Or possibly a clunk," said Ulff.

Darnell stayed silent.

We stood for a moment, not daring to move. But we heard nothing more.

Finally, the prince gave himself a good shake.

"'Twas only our imaginations," he said. "Let us not dawdle. We have children to find."

He took a step—and tumbled over a tangled root.

Ulff put out a hand to help him up, but the prince waved him off.

"Now we know the root's there," he said, "we can avoid it in the future."

He climbed to his feet, righted his helmet, and set off once more down the path.

After a snort, a stomp, and a few tugs on his reins from the prince, Darnell followed.

Ulff and I trailed behind.

At long last, we came to a clearing. In the center sat a neat brown cottage.

"Would you look at that," said Ulff.

We stared, all four of us, even Darnell. I'd never seen so much gingerbread. Gingerbread walls. Gingerbread doors. Gingerbread roof. Even the shutters were slices of gingerbread. Gumdrops lined the house, and the whole thing was held together by something creamy and swirly and white.

"Is that . . . frosting?" My stomach let out a growl.

"With sprinkles," said Ulff.

Charming nodded grimly. "The witch's house."

"The witch's house? No fooling?" Ulff shook his head. "A wicked old witch in a cottage this sweet . . . I never would've thought it."

"How do you think she lures in children?" said the prince.

He tethered Darnell to a candy cane porch rail, and we started toward the door.

As we reached the porch, the spicy sweetness of the gingerbread folded around me. My stomach rumbled. My head grew light. I hadn't eaten anything since a tough bit of gristle the night before. But now I had to cross my arms over my chest to keep from ripping a marshmallow off a window box and stuffing it in my mouth.

"Lookee there." Ulff pointed at an apple resting on the bottom step. "All these candies and sweets, and

116

smack in the middle, a healthy bit of fruit. I guess it's true what they say. You can't live on gingerbread alone."

"Interesting." Charming snatched the apple from the step. He held it up to the light.

"Stop!" a voice rang out. "Don't eat that!"

17

A Crack in the Gingerbread

𝔄 young woman hurried around the corner of the cottage. A cloud of flour wafted from out of her apron. A bonnet billowed about her head like a puff pastry.

"Don't!" She reached for the apple.

"Why not?" Charming held the apple close to his breastplate. "Is it poisoned?"

Darnell had been licking the candy cane porch rail. Though when he heard the word "poisoned," he stopped mid-lick.

The young woman frowned. She was out of breath, her face flushed pink.

"Of course not," she said. "It's just not yet ripe."

Charming studied the apple. "It certainly *looks* ripe."

Ulff nodded. "A nice healthy red all over."

"You can't judge a fruit by its peel." The young woman plucked the apple from Charming's hand. "When it ripens, I'll bake it into a nice pie. But it's no good now."

"Bake into a pie." The prince considered this. He turned to me. "Make a note. If I'm right, and I believe I

am, this woman is none other than"—he turned back to her—"the witch."

"Well . . . yes." She slid the apple into her apron pocket. "Isn't that why you're here?"

Ulff stared at the young woman, then at the cottage, then back at the woman. "You don't look like a witch. You—you—" He gulped. "You're lovely."

The woman flushed a deeper pink. "Thank you," she said. "You're quite kind."

Ulff flushed, too, a bristly red.

Charming set his jaw in a steely line. "You can't judge a fruit by its peel, Ulff."

"I'm just surprised you came so soon," said the witch. "I didn't think anyone knew. No one ventures out this way much."

"No, I don't suppose they do." The prince studied the clearing. "Lonely. Far from the village. The perfect spot to commit a crime."

"Exactly," said the witch. "Do you want to see the damage?"

Charming, Ulff, and I looked at each other.

"Damage?" said the prince.

"The worst is out back," she said.

She was already making her way along the peanut brittle walk. We followed. When she reached the rear of the cottage, she pointed to one of the windows.

Charming stared at it. "Great gobsmacking ghost! The kingdom is simply plagued with crime. Rings, children, letters, crumbs—"

"Feathers," said Ulff.

"—feathers. And now this." The prince waved an armored hand at the cottage. "A gingerbread vandal."

Ulff ran his hand over the crumbled edge of a shutter. "It's terrible."

It was. The shutter was broken. The top half dangled by a thin line of frosting. The bottom half was gone.

The licorice trim had been torn from the frame and the window box cracked, its marshmallows missing.

I reached out to touch the smeared frosting, then stopped myself. I didn't think it would be polite to lick my fingers in front of the witch.

I folded my arms over my chest. "When did this happen?" I said.

The witch shook her head. "Sometime in the night. Everything was fine when I went to bed. But this morning"—she raised her hands—"I found *this*."

Ulff nodded. "Same as the children. Fine when they went to bed. Gone the next morning."

"Children?" said the witch.

"A young girl and her brother." Charming motioned to me, and I pulled out my sketches. "Have you seen them?"

The witch studied the drawings.

"Ah, Hansel and Gretel," she said.

"So you *do* have them," said the prince. "I knew it!"

"No." The witch shook her head. "I've seen them in the forest with their father. But they never come near here. Their mother won't allow it. What would *I* want with them?"

"You're the witch," said Charming. "You lure children with sweets, then push them into your oven. We've heard the rumors."

The witch sighed. "Who do you think started those rumors?"

The prince frowned, confused.

"I live in a gingerbread house," she said. "If I didn't do something to protect myself, this kind of thing"—she waved a hand at the broken shingle—"would happen all the time."

I nodded. "People would eat you out of house and home. Truly."

The prince narrowed his eyes. "So why live in gingerbread at all?"

"Why?" The witch blinked in surprise. "Wouldn't you, if you could? Wouldn't everyone?"

"I would," said Ulff.

My stomach let out a growl of agreement.

The witch turned to me. Her voice was soft. "I craft my cottage with care. I use the finest flour, the purest spice. I mix and roll and bake with tenderness, then frost with love. To see it torn apart like this, it—it—"

She touched my cheek. Her fingertips were warm against my skin.

"—it breaks my heart," she said.

A tear welled up in her eye. She pressed her sweet, sugary cheek against the top of my head and wrapped an arm around me.

No one ever hugged a Swill. We didn't even hug each other.

"We'll find whoever did this," I heard myself whisper. "I promise."

18

A Bag Full of Men

It was nice of her to pack us a light snack for our journey." Ulff stuffed a whole gingerbread man into his mouth. "I'll have to visit her cottage again soon to thank her properly."

We'd left the forest and were making our way back through Twigg. The witch had given us a bag of gingerbread men, warm from her oven.

I pulled off the tip of my little man's shoe and popped it into my mouth.

Charming gripped his own cookie in his armored hand. But he hadn't taken so much as a nibble. He led Darnell by the reins. Darnell reached out his tongue and licked a bit of frosting off the prince's gingerbread.

"She may have bewitched the two of you," said Charming. We clopped past the shoemaker's shop. "But I've seen a bit more of this world, and her trickery won't work so well on me. A mysterious apple. All that gingerbread. She says she's not trying to enchant children, yet she lives in a cottage that's enchantingly delicious. It all smells a bit fishy."

"Smells like gingerbread to me. Besides," said Ulff, "you were suspicious of the stepmother not that long ago."

"Yes." The prince turned to us with a sudden thought. "What if they're in it together?"

"The witch and the stepmother?" I swallowed my gingerbread. "Seems doubtful."

Ulff dug out another cookie from the bag. "The stepmother won't let her children anywhere near that lovely woman in the forest. Both of them said so."

The prince thought about this.

"Unless!" He raised a finger. "Unless they said it simply to throw us off the scent."

"I don't know," I said. "When anybody in Twigg so much as sneezes, the whole village is there to wipe their nose. Nothing much gets past them. If the witch and Mrs. Woodcutter were plotting together, I think someone would've noticed."

128

"And would've said so, too," Ulff mumbled. "Twigg folk love nothing better than to snitch each other out."

"True." Charming sighed. "I suppose they're both innocent."

"Well—" I hesitated.

Charming narrowed his eyes. "Well what?"

"Well," I said. "Mrs. Woodcutter would never harm Hansel and Gretel. Of that, I'm sure. But I think she knows something, something she was afraid to tell us, something about"—I took a breath—"crumbs."

Ulff stopped chewing. "She *did* seem nervous at the mention of them."

I nodded. "And nervous as well when we asked if anything else was missing."

Charming thought about this. "Do you think she knew about the missing crumb trail?"

"Or the missing letter?" said Ulff.

"*Or*"—Charming raised an eyebrow—"perhaps she's the one who took them both!"

"I did spy some loose crumbs on her doorstep," I admitted. "But what reason would she have?"

"Maybe she was hungry," said Ulff. "Maybe she saw the crumbs and couldn't help herself. Maybe she gobbled them up, saw she'd eaten the only thing that would lead her to her children, and couldn't bear to tell anyone."

"Maybe." I took another bite of my little man. "But what about the letter?"

Ulff grunted. "She must've been truly hungry to eat that."

"I can't think my father's letter would be that tasty," said Charming.

We turned past the clockmaker's at the end of the lane.

"Who else do we have?" said the prince.

I licked sugar from my fingers and pulled out my notes. "There's Mr. Stiltskin."

"Stiltskin." The prince spun this thought in his mind. "What do we know of him?"

Ulff shrugged. "Lurks about here and there. Pops up when you least expect it. Has a nose for crumbs."

And he was rambling through the village that morning about the time Hansel and Gretel vanished.

But I couldn't say that. I couldn't say I'd been perched on the roof of Swill hovel, admiring the luster of the king's ring, when I happened to hear the peddler jangling up the high street.

I blinked. Jangling. *Jangling.* I nearly dropped my gingerbread man.

"That's what we heard in the woods!" I said. "When the birds startled."

"The clunk?" said Ulff.

"The clang?" said the prince.

"The clink." I nodded. "The peddler clinks and clangs."

"And rattles and plinks, truly." Ulff frowned. "But he

wouldn't be in the forest. He disappeared with the rest of the village—*pffft*—at the first mention of it."

"Unless"—the prince wrestled this thought—"unless that's what he *wanted* us to think. The peddler pretended to disappear—then followed us."

We took a moment to ponder this.

"But why?" Ulff said finally.

"Why?" said the prince. "Well, because—because—" He sighed. "I don't know why."

By this time, we'd passed through Twigg and were nearing the hovel once more. Charming slowed to a stop. He reached into his gauntlet, poked this way and that, and finally took the whole thing off and shook it.

He stared at the empty piece of armor. "And now I've gone and lost our lucky mitten."

"Are you sure?" Ulff took the gauntlet from him and gave it another good shake. When nothing fell out, he handed the gauntlet back. "It wasn't giving us much luck anyway."

The prince sighed and slid the gauntlet back onto his hand.

Behind us on the roadway, I spied a line of dark brown bits of gingerbread, the scattered leftovers of Ulff's enthusiastic munching. Birds were, indeed, flitting down to feast on them, just as the dwarfs had thought.

I pointed. "There's a trail of crumbs for you," I said, thinking to lighten the mood.

"Yes." Charming nodded. "Sadly, it only leads to Ulff."

He stood in the roadway, staring up at the castle.

"We're no closer to finding those youngsters than when we set out," he said. "How can I face my father? This was my chance—*finally*—to show him I'm a worthy heir."

"You're his son," I said. "Of course you're worthy."

"I try to believe that," said Charming. "But some of my father's council aren't convinced. Chief among them, Sir Roderick."

He clanked down on a log beside the road. Darnell

leaned over to nuzzle the prince's cheek. The prince absentmindedly scratched his faithful steed behind his ears.

"I'll bet Sir Roderick was none too pleased when your father put you in charge of the castle," said Ulff.

"One would think." Charming frowned. "And at first, he *did* seem unconvinced. But once he gave it a ponder, he agreed it was a sensible plan. In fact, he urged my father to go through with it. In the end, he was on my side."

I nodded. Sir Roderick had acted much the same way at the palace when the prince asked to lead the search for Hansel and Gretel. He'd first objected, then thought better of it. But he didn't seem to really be on the prince's side through any of it.

The prince sighed. "Many of the council say I'd be a disaster for the kingdom. I'm not sure they're wrong." He stared down forlornly at his helmet. "I couldn't even protect my poor plume."

"You're a fine prince," said Ulff, "plume or no plume. You're tall. You have good manners. And you keep your armor nice and shiny. What more could anyone want?"

Charming shrugged one shiny, armored shoulder. "Some think Sir Roderick would be the better choice. He's my father's cousin, you know?"

"A cousin can't be his heir," I said. "First, there's you." I counted on my fingers. "Then your sister."

Charming nodded. "Angelica. But she's even younger than I am. Many of the council say *too* young. And after Angelica, well . . . there's Roderick."

"Roderick." Ulff shuddered. "That's one fellow I'll never call—"

"Your Highness!" a voice thundered toward us from the roadway.

I froze. I was standing in the grass, on the far side of Darnell. I forced myself to steal a peek at the sound from under the faithful steed's belly.

A stout man lumbered toward us. His heavy boots

thudded over the packed dirt. He stopped before he reached us and leaned over, hands on his knees, to catch his breath.

"It's my boy," he panted. "My youngest."

He kept his distance and stayed downwind. But he looked at the prince with pleading eyes.

"He's gone," he said.

I swallowed.

The man was my father.

19

A Fog in the Roadway

I didn't mean to hide from him.

Not really.

But Darnell wasn't just faithful. He was enormous. His haunches stood a good foot higher than my head. When my father lumbered up, I was on the other side of the enormous steed, puzzling through my notes. My father didn't see me.

And when I heard his voice, I just stood there, hands clamped to the pages, a great woozy fog clamping my head. The prince could've reached out and tipped me over, and I wouldn't have been able to raise an arm to break my fall.

Somewhere through the fog, I heard Ulff whisper, "It's the dung farmer, Your Highness. Goes by the name of Swill."

Darnell swung his big head toward my father, then toward me. He snorted and flicked his tail.

I heard Charming clank to his feet. "Ah, yes. That explains"—he sniffed—"a lot. You do a fine job with our latrines, Mr. Swill. Now, what is it you were saying about your son?"

I heard my father take a wheezing breath.

And I should have said something. Right there and then.

But any words that might have tumbled from my mouth stayed frozen in my throat, nearly choking me.

"He came home with his brothers last night." My father's voice quivered. "But this morning—"

His voice broke.

I swallowed. I never thought I'd be gone long enough for anyone to miss me. In fact, I never thought anyone would miss me no matter how long I was gone. Except maybe Snout and Gerald, who'd have a fistfight to see who would have to pull the cart.

"I should've stayed with him," my father said. "I should've made sure he was safe in his bed. He's

nothing but bones, that one. Not a speck of meat on him. If he's out there, somewhere, he's got no way to defend himself."

I heard the rattle of armor. I peered again under Darnell's belly.

Even with the stench billowing off my father's clothing and the flies buzzing about his beard, Charming had clasped an arm around his shoulders.

"Worry not," Charming told him. "We will search. We will scour. We will sweep the kingdom from end to end. I speak for the king when I say this. We *will* find your son."

My father wiped a ham-sized fist across his wet eyes.

"Thank you," he said.

He turned and trudged back up the roadway, his shoulders slumped beneath his crusty tunic.

I wanted to run after him. I wanted to tell him I wasn't lost.

But I stood there, unmoving, for so long, it seemed as if my very feet had sprouted into the ground. I had this wild thought that as long as I didn't move, no one would know I was standing there. They'd see me as just one more tree swaying by the roadside.

Charming gave a heavy sigh. "Add this to our list. This missing boy, this—" He frowned. "What did the dung farmer say his son's name was?"

"He didn't," said Ulff. "There's a whole pack of 'em living in Swill Cottage. Don't know that any of them have proper names."

"Yes, they do," I said. My voice surprised even me.

Charming, Ulff, and Darnell turned to look at me.

"I mean, they must," I said. "Nobody goes around without a name."

Ulff squinched his face and nodded. "That's true. They have to call each other something. Otherwise, they'd get all mixed up. I don't guess the villagers ever get close enough to sort out which one is which.

Everyone just calls them Those Swills."

I swallowed something hard in my throat, and it wasn't gingerbread.

Those Swills.

I'd heard that plenty of times. I'd even said it myself.

It sounded worse coming from Ulff.

"Write that down for now," Charming told me. "I imagine we'll learn his true name sooner or later."

No. They wouldn't. Before we got back to the castle, I would slip away. I would wait till no one was looking, then disappear into the trees. I would hightail it back to the hovel and smear dung over my face and tunic. Ulff and the prince would never know who I was.

I straightened my notes and started to scribble *Swill boy—missing.*

Before I could finish, a trumpet sounded.

"Hear ye! Hear ye!" The town crier's voice rang out.

"Sweet Nellie's nightshirt." the prince ran an armored hand over his eyes. "What now?"

"The kidnapper has been found," cried the crier. "The king's men have arrested—"

Charming, Ulff, and I leaned forward, waiting. Even Darnell pricked up his ears.

"—the troll."

20

A Smudge on the Rail

"The troll!" Charming thunked a hand against his unplumed helmet. "Of course! He was under the bridge the whole time. And I never even thought to question him." He paced one way, then another, armor clattering. "Foolish, foolish, foo—"

"He didn't do it," I said.

Charming stopped. Ulff quit chewing a cookie mid-crunch. Darnell turned his head toward me.

"I mean—" I was doing a fair bit of pacing myself.

I had to save the troll.

And also keep my identity secret.

And somehow let my father know I was safe.

And keep my identity secret.

And also save the troll.

"I mean, how do they *know* he did it?" I said. "There's no evidence."

"Of course there's evidence," said the prince. "There must be. The king's men don't go off willy-nilly, arresting trolls without evidence."

Darnell snorted.

Ulff almost choked on his gingerbread.

"This morning, they were about to go off willy-nilly to upend the village looking for the king's ring," he said. "I know because I wanted to go with them."

"Yes. See? Right there." I flung a hand toward Ulff. "They might *not* have evidence. And if they don't—"

"If they don't"—the prince narrowed his eyes— "they're arresting an innocent troll." He gave a sharp nod. "To the bridge!"

He made a bounding leap at Darnell.

Hit the saddle and bounced off with a thundering *clank!*

He picked himself up.

Leaped.

Clanked.

Finally, with Ulff crouched on all fours to give him a boost and me braced on the other side to keep him from sliding off, the prince climbed aboard his faithful steed.

"To the bridge!" Charming spurred Darnell, and they set off. Darnell's hooves pounded the roadway, churning a cloud of dust.

Ulff and I coughed and bolted after them.

When we huffed up to the bridge a few minutes later, the dust had settled. A few villagers had arrived ahead of us. Others trickled in behind.

The prince had managed to dismount. He was talking with the captain of the King's Men, his face knotted in a grave frown.

"Sir Roderick sent us," the captain was telling him. "He suspected the troll all along."

Charming narrowed his eyes. "On what evidence?"

The captain waved a hand toward a long red smudge on the bridge rail.

Charming strode to the rail. He dabbed a finger in the smudge. He lifted it to his nose and gave a sniff.

Ulff swallowed. "Is it . . . ?"

The prince gave a grim nod. "Frosting."

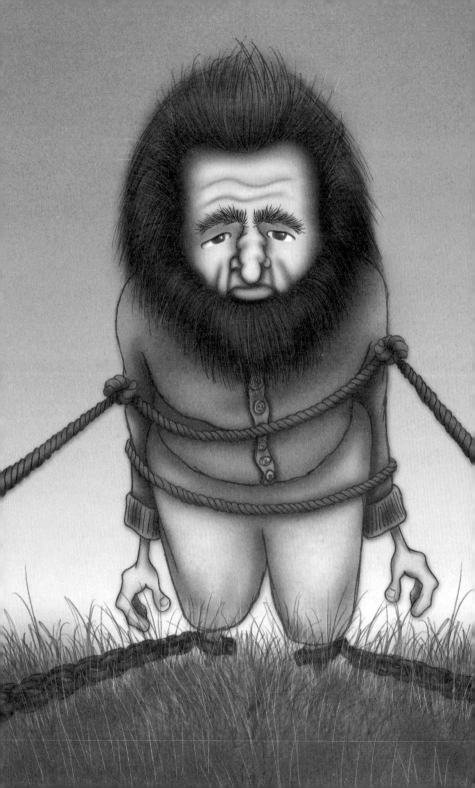

The villagers gasped.

Ulff stared at the smudge. "So it was the *troll* who wrecked the gingerbread?"

"It certainly looks that way," said Charming. "And if he wrecked the gingerbread, he's likely behind the other crimes as well."

"Not necessarily," I said. "I mean, maybe he got hungry. Maybe he ate the witch's shutter. That doesn't mean—"

"Make way!"

A troop of the King's Men sloshed up from the stream below.

Between them, they had the troll. Ropes bound his hulking shoulders. Chains shackled his legs. His huge, shaggy head was bent, and the chains rattled with each step he took.

He turned his eyes toward me. They were huge and yellow and shot through with veins.

But they didn't look awful.

They looked sad.

He gave me a long look. Then he turned his eyes to the ground again as the guards pushed him toward the castle.

"No!" I pleaded with the prince. "They can't arrest him. He wouldn't take Hansel and Gretel. He wouldn't. He could've taken me, but he didn't. He—he saved my life."

The prince put a hand on my shoulder. "They have evidence."

"About the gingerbread, maybe." I looked desperately from the prince to the troll and back again. "But not about the other things. Not about Hansel and Gretel. Not about—"

"Yes. They do." The prince gave me a sad smile. "Or at least, they will. He did it, Nobbin."

"Nobbin?" A stout man lumbered up behind the last stragglers from the village.

He stopped.

He stared at me.

"Son?" said my father.

21

A Lump in the Throat

𝕿he world stopped.

For one long, terrible moment, the villagers stopped talking. Ulff stopped chewing. The very birds in the trees stopped chirping.

One word echoed through the silence: *son*.

"But . . ." Ulff looked from me to my father and back again, his face crumpled in confusion. "You told me you weren't from around here. You said you were just . . . Nobbin."

"*Just* . . . Nobbin?" Confusion creased my father's face, too. "You told them you weren't a Swill?"

"No," I said. "I never said I wasn't a Swill. I just said I was"—I swallowed—"nobody."

"Nobody." My father's voice was more of a rasp than a roar. "The name was good enough for my father and my father's father and his father before him. But you'd rather be"—he shook his head—"nobody."

He looked at me for a long moment. Then he turned and marched back down the road.

I started after him.

But I could still hear the troll's chains clanking in the distance. The world may have stopped, but the King's Men hadn't. They marched on, the troll bound between them. They had topped the hill and nearly reached the castle.

I turned toward Ulff. He lowered his head.

I turned toward the prince. He stood staring up at the castle.

"I'm a Swill," I told him. "It's true." I swallowed the lump that strangled my throat. "That's why you have to listen to me. I cross this bridge every night. Last night, I lost my footing and plunged into the stream. I thought I was a goner. Even my brothers thought so. But the troll—he saved me. He didn't hurt me. He didn't eat me. He saved my life. He would never take Hansel and Gretel. You have to believe that."

The prince didn't look at me. He slid his helmet onto his head, started to straighten the plume, remembered it wasn't there, and let his hand drop to his side.

I looked at Ulff. And the villagers.

No one met my eyes.

Even Darnell snorted and turned his head.

I stared at the ground. They were right. How could they take the word of a lying, stinking, cheating, double-crossing, no-good coward of a dung farmer's son?

22

A Messenger on the Stoop

Jf my father heard my footsteps scuffing along the roadway behind him, he gave no sign. I caught up to him just as he reached the hovel. He stopped short, and I nearly ran into him.

Standing on our stoop was a messenger outfitted in the king's livery. He had his back to us, his gloved hand raised to rap on our rickety door.

"May I help you?" my father's voice rumbled across the dirt patch.

The messenger started. He turned, saw my father, and snapped his heels together. With a flourish, he held out a rolled parchment, tied with a ribbon of royal purple.

My father eyed the messenger. He eyed the parchment. Finally, he reached for it. He snatched off the ribbon, unfurled the message, and squinched his eyes. He grunted and murmured, "Hmmm," as if giving a good long thought to whatever the message said.

I knew better. My father had no idea what the message said. But he would squint a hole in that parchment before he let the king's messenger suspect he couldn't read.

"You forgot your glasses," I said quietly. "I could read it for you. So you don't give yourself a headache trying to squint."

My father flicked a glance at me, then at the messenger, then back at me. He handed me the whole bundle. I slipped the ribbon over my wrist for safekeeping and smoothed out the parchment.

It was a letter from the king.

It was short.

To: Master Swill
      Swill Cottage

Due to recent troubling events involving the urchin boy, Nobbin, your services as royal dung farmer are no longer needed.

This termination takes effect immediately and applies to your sons, your sons' sons, and their sons after them.

Regally,
His Majesty the King

23

A Traitor on the Roof

𝕴 hunkered on the roof of the hovel, fiddling with the purple ribbon on my wrist.

Moonlight shone over the dirt patch below. My father leaned against the dung cart. He patted its splintery rails and let out a sigh. Lout hugged his shovel. Snout cradled a bucket in his arms. Gerald started first this way, then that, not sure what to do.

I'd thought being a dung farmer was the worst thing anyone could be.

I was wrong.

Being a dung farmer with no dung to farm—*that* was the worst thing.

Being a dung farmer's son who had betrayed everyone?

Even worse still.

"Blast it!" Lout pounded his shovel against the ground. "I'm a Swill. I was born to shovel. If I can't shovel dung, I'll—I'll shovel"—he choked back a gag—"dirt."

"Dirt?"

Snout shuddered. Gerald covered his mouth. My father had to look away.

Lout sank the blade of his shovel into the ground. He turned over a spadeful of dirt and dumped it into Snout's bucket. Snout looked at it for a moment, shook his head, and passed it to Gerald. Gerald heaved the dirt into the cart, handed the bucket back to Snout, and the whole thing started again.

Dig.

Pass.

Dump.

Dig.

Pass.

Dump.

Soon, the dirt patch was pocked with holes, our cart filled with dirt.

My brothers stood there, looking at it.

Then Gerald began scooping the dirt out of the cart. He handed the bucket to Snout, who passed it to Lout, who began filling the holes.

My father rested his elbows on the cart. He stared up at the castle and gave a great, heaving sigh. The whole cart shuddered.

He'd have been better off if I *had* gone missing— and never found. He'd still have his dung. He'd still have the king's trust. I sank back against the chimney. He *wouldn't* have a letter on the king's own parchment, sealed by the king's own—

I sat up. My father's letter had been written on the king's own parchment. I glanced at the ribbon on my wrist. But it had *not* been sealed by the king's own ring.

Not to mention, it had been delivered so quick. Before we got back to the hovel even.

How did the king find out so soon? How did news of the urchin boy reach his ears—and then his pen—so fast? And why had he secured it with a ribbon rather than a wax seal, stamped with his very own ring?

I stopped.

Urchin. I'd been called that once before.

And not by the king.

By someone who *couldn't* seal my father's letter with the king's own ring. Someone who may have taken the king's ring once, but did not have it now. Not since my urchin self had returned it to its rightful owner.

I thought of another letter, the woodcutter's, and how it had gone missing at the same time as his children.

166

I thought of the witch, and what Charming had said of her: She wasn't trying to enchant children, yet she lived in a cottage that was enchantingly delicious.

I thought of the crumbs on the woodcutter's doorstep. And of Ulff's trail of crumbs on the roadway. Ulff's were the same dark brown—the brown of gingerbread—but they were not a trail for us to follow. They were a trail left behind as we paid scant attention.

I thought of the cold of the castle, and how it must vex the king. And of how he would be that much more vexed with no one shoveling his dung.

As I thought all these thoughts, I turned my gaze toward the moonlit castle.

And suddenly . . . I knew.

I knew why the king's letter came so quickly. I knew how the woodcutter's letter had disappeared. I knew who stole the king's ring. I knew who wrecked the witch's cottage. I knew where the red smear on the bridge came from.

I knew what happened to Hansel and Gretel.

24

A Clank at the Gate

The gatehouse door stretched into the darkness above me. I could just make out the heavy iron knocker that hung above my head.

I leaped and batted at it. A loud *CLANK!* echoed through the gatehouse.

I waited.

I leaped and clanked once more.

Finally, the little hatch squeaked open. Ulff squinted out. Moonlight shone over his bristly face.

169

"Down here," I said.

He pulled his eyeglasses from his sleeve, slid them on, and finally picked me out of the shadows.

"Oh." He started to close the hatch.

"Wait!" I said. "I need to see the king."

"That's what you said last time."

"It's important."

"You said that last time, too."

"But I have—"

"A talent for finding things, I know." His voice caught in his throat. "All it found *me* was a heap of trouble."

He gave me a long look, slid his glasses back into his sleeve, and swung the hatch shut. I heard the bolt click into place.

I leaped and clanked the knocker. I leaped and clanked again. I kept leaping and clanking until I collapsed in a heap on the cobbled path, trying to catch my breath.

I had to save the troll.

And find Hansel and Gretel.

And help the prince.

And find Hansel and Gretel.

And save the troll.

I stared up at the thick wooden door.

How could I do any of it if I couldn't get in?

25

A Shinny up the Chute

$\mathfrak{H}$ere's a funny thing about the castle. The king posted sentries at the gates. He stationed lookouts on the battlements.

He never thought to guard the toilets.

I shot a quick glance at the gatehouse to make sure Ulff wasn't peeking out from the hatch. Then I skidded down the embankment and along the castle wall to the dung pit.

The blessed, lovely dung pit.

The stench of it filled the darkness. Flies buzzed about in a thick horde.

I swatted them away and circled the pit to the small hole in the stone wall of the tower, just above my head.

The dung chute.

I reached up into it. I found solid handholds in the rough stone. I dug my fingers in, gave a couple good bounces on the balls of my feet, and hiked myself into the stone passage. I wedged my feet and shoulders against the stone and began climbing.

There was a reason the king hadn't thought to guard the toilets. Anyone bigger than the dung farmer's youngest son would never have fit into them. The air was thick and the chute dark. I couldn't even see the stone wall that was rubbing my very nose.

I tipped my head back to gulp in a breath and spied a pinprick of gray light far above.

I climbed toward it. The pinprick grew larger, then larger still, until it was the size of a dinner plate. I reached up, gave one last heave, and popped through the seat of the king's toilet.

Uncle Bert's galoshes! The rumors were true.

Hanging about the garderobe were peg after peg of the king's robes and cloaks and gowns. Moonlight sliced through a narrow window and tippled off the silk, fur, and gold-stitched velvet.

A tall cupboard held the king's smaller things. Gloves. Stockings. Shoes.

And a tray of the king's jewels.

Even in the dim light, they shimmered. I tiptoed toward them.

In the very center glittered a gold ring, covered

in jewels—green, blue, and, the largest, a deep red.
The king's signet ring. The very ring I'd fished from
the dung.

I traced my finger over the lion carved into its face.

The king hadn't lost it down the dung chute.

But I knew who had.

26

A Prowl Through the Castle

A narrow door led from the garderobe. I slipped through into a cold, dark room. In the shadows, I could make out an enormous, canopied bed hung with heavy, gold-threaded draperies.

I was in the king's bedchamber.

I froze. At this time of night, surely the king must be in his bed.

But if he were, he was a much quieter sleeper than any I was used to. I did not hear the snores and

snuffling and rolling and wrestling of a night spent with Swills. In fact, I heard nothing at all.

I crept closer, my boots making scarcely a sound on the thick rug. I peered into the bed. Behind the draperies, the bedclothes lay smooth and flat.

The king was not there.

I allowed myself to let out the lungful of breath I'd been holding, then tiptoed across the room. I eased open the massive door, listened, heard nothing, and crept from the chamber.

On the journey up the hill to the castle, I'd made a plan, such as it was. I would steal into the night-darkened throne room, choose a spot behind a pillar or tapestry to hide myself away for the night, then make my case to the king in the morning, when he took to his throne to hold court. I would make my case fast, before he threw me out.

Or into the dungeon.

But first, I had to *find* the throne room. I wound

my way down a circular stairway. Torches set into the wall cast looming shadows around me. The stairs were easier to navigate than the dung chute. Still, there was nothing here but me and the steps and the solid stone walls. I peered around the curve of the stairway. If I happened upon a servant or a lord or lady, I had nowhere to hide.

I crept to the archway at the bottom and poked my head out.

The stairs opened onto a long hallway. Wooden doors set into the stone walls marched down the passage on both sides. Bedchambers, I guessed. One of the doors was open, and a large woven basket filled with laundry stood outside. I could hear the laundress inside the chamber, huffing and heaving and mumbling to herself. Wrestling clean bedclothes onto a mattress, no doubt.

I turned the other way. Two of the king's men marched toward me down the hall.

I jerked my head back and scrambled up the steps, around a curve where I was sure the king's men couldn't spy me.

I hugged the wall tightly, my heart pounding, and listened.

The thud of boots came closer.

And closer.

I held my breath.

The boots thudded past and faded down the hall.

I started to breathe again.

But before the last thud of boot steps could die out, voices echoed down the stairway. I froze. The voices grew louder. They were coming toward me.

I skittered down the steps and poked my head through the archway once more.

I looked one way. The laundry basket still stood sentry outside the open door.

I looked the other. The king's men were gone, but now a footman strode toward me. He carried an

enormous tea tray, his face hidden behind a tall silver
teapot.

The voices above grew closer.

The footman below was nearly upon me.

I turned, thinking to scuttle past the open
doorway—and the laundress—before footman or voices
caught up to me—

—only to glimpse the laundress herself heading from
the bedchamber, carrying a heap of dirty bedclothes.

I looked one way, then the other—

—and dove into the laundry basket.

27

A Boy in a Basket

I curled up in a ball beneath the wrinkled linens, not moving, not blinking, not daring to breathe.

Footsteps thumped past. I heard one voice, then another, muffled by the laundry draped around my head, and more footsteps.

As these steps passed, I heard a grunt, and something landed above me in the basket. The laundress had dumped the second heap of laundry onto the first, crushing my face into the linens below.

I clamped shut my lips to hold back a sputter.

The basket rocked to one side, then the other, before the whole thing, with me inside, was hoisted into the air.

"Cor!" I heard a woman's voice groan. "Laundry do get heavy. And smelly."

I took a quiet sniff of my sleeve. She was right. It no longer smelled like sleeve. It smelled like dung chute.

The bedclothes and I bounced and jounced as she carried us off through the castle. We turned one way, then another, the basket bumping so wildly I thought I would well and truly come flying out the top of it.

Then it stopped. The basket dropped to the floor. A grunt escaped my throat, but the laundress grunted at the same time, mingling the two grunts together.

A door hinge squeaked, and the laundress's footsteps thumped away.

I peeked from under the linens.

The basket and I were in a hallway outside another bedchamber. The laundress had gone inside.

I wrested myself from the laundry, pulling a pillowcase from my shoulder and a stray stocking from around my head.

I was in the wide opening of a passageway where one hall crossed another. Tapestries draped the walls, and pillars stood sentry at the corners.

As I crouched there, once more trying to think which way to go—and four directions to choose from this time—I heard footsteps. Again.

Grandad's girdle, but this was a busy castle. Did no one here sleep?

I scuttled out of sight behind a pillar.

"I already told Sir Roderick," a voice echoed down the passage. "I'd never set eyes on the troll till you dragged him from the stream."

The footsteps grew louder.

I peeked from behind the pillar.

Two of the king's men trooped toward me. They marched a short fellow between them, gripping him by the elbows. He was round and red and bristly and wore a lumpy leather cap.

Ulff.

I held my breath as they passed. I waited a moment, then fell in behind them, hugging the wall as I tiptoed in their wake.

They turned a corner. I squeezed around the corner after them. They marched through a doorway. I tucked through the doorway on their heels. They snaked up one passage and down another, turning left, then right, then left again. I followed, pressing myself into the shadows. When they marched through an archway, I slipped in behind them—

—and found myself in the throne room.

It was not the dark, shadowy place I had expected this time of night. Light blazed from the chandeliers. Lords and ladies ringed the edge. The witch was there. And so was Mr. Stiltskin.

As they parted to allow the king's men through, I

saw the troll hunched in the center of the room. His huge yellow eyes stared at the marble floor. His massive shoulders sagged beneath the weight of the chains that bound him.

Charming sagged nearby, his normally square shoulders slumped in their armor. His head was low, his mood lower. He'd replaced his plume with a goose feather, but the stubby gray quill dangled sideways on his head and only served to point out that his magnificent crimson plume was gone—along with every speck of his confidence. Even his armor seemed dull.

The woodcutter stood to the side, his arm around his wife. They sagged against each other.

The king, rubbing at the knot of worry between his eyes, seemed to sag in his throne at the top of the marble steps.

Sir Roderick stood beside him, arms crossed, upper lip trying not to curl into a smile.

The king's men thrust Ulff before the steps. He

stumbled, but managed to right himself. He pulled off his cap and gave the king a low bow.

"Father." The prince approached and placed a hand on Ulff's shoulder. "This man is a faithful guard. I can vouch for his character. I spent all this long day with him."

"Yes." The word slithered from Sir Roderick's mouth. "Perhaps your day would have been better spent tending to the squirrels in the pantry."

Charming stared at him. "Ulff is a fine companion, and I would welcome his company when I tend to those scratching noises that—that—"

"Aren't even squirrels," I said in a loud whisper.

"—aren't even squirrels," finished the prince. He stopped, eyes wide as he realized what he'd just said.

"Not squirrels?" The king leaned forward in his throne. "Are you sure?"

"I—" The prince hesitated. He shot a glance over his shoulder and spied me lurking behind a lady's wide silk skirts.

The lady spied me, too, wrinkled her nose, and
moved away.

"Positive," I whispered.

The prince turned back to his father. He swallowed.
"I'm positive."

"Your *Majesty*." Sir Roderick turned to the king.
"The prince is clearly—"

"Because the scratching," I whispered.

"Because the scratching," said the prince.

"—is none other—"

"—is none other—"

"—than Hansel and Gretel," I whispered.

"—than—" The prince turned now and gave me a puzzled look.

I nodded.

The prince turned back. He squared his shoulders. He leveled his gaze at Sir Roderick.

"The scratching noises," said Charming, "were made by Hansel and Gretel."

28

A Secret in the Pantry

The Woodcutters gasped. The troll lifted his head. The lords and ladies began talking at once.

"Your *Majesty*." Sir Roderick's voice was smooth, but his eyes blazed. "The prince is listening to this urchin again and—"

But the king had already risen from his throne and marched down the marble steps.

The prince led the way, through a passage, down a narrow stairway, and into the kitchen. Ulff followed close behind, hands tensed, ready to tip the prince back onto his feet should he go tail over teakettle. But the prince did not tumble or stumble once.

He stopped at the pantry, and we crowded behind him: the king, the woodcutter, his wife, the witch, Mr. Stiltskin, Ulff, me, and even the troll, led by the pair of king's men. Lords and ladies pressed in behind. Sir Roderick hovered at the edge of the crowd.

"And now, I shall reveal what happened," said Charming. He flicked a nervous glance at me.

I nodded and began whispering furtively. The prince listened, then explained it in his princely way.

"Hansel and Gretel saw the letter," I whispered.

"Young Gretel and her small brother Hansel," said the prince, "saw the letter from the king dismissing their father as royal woodcutter."

"Dismissing the woodcutter?" The king frowned. "I wrote no such letter."

"No," said the prince. "But someone did."

Ulff gave a grim nod. "Someone who snatched His Majesty's royal ring to stamp the letter with his royal seal, I'll wager."

"And wrote another letter dismissing the dung farmer," I whispered.

"And wrote another letter dismissing . . ." Charming stopped. He frowned at me. "Truly?" he said.

I nodded.

Charming turned to his father. "And wrote another letter to the dung farmer, informing him his dung-scooping services would no longer be needed."

"Good heavens!" said the king.

"Treachery!" said one of the king's men.

"We'll probably never know who did it," said Sir Roderick. His voice sounded strangled.

The king studied Roderick for a long moment. "I imagine we'll find out. Eventually."

Sir Roderick's mouth had gaped open. Now he snapped it shut and swallowed hard.

I continued my whisper. "Hansel and Gretel heard their parents talking. . . ."

Charming nodded. "The Woodcutters worried they wouldn't be able to feed their family. The youngsters heard them talking. They sneaked into the forest. They broke off the witch's shingle. They brought it back to their cottage so their parents wouldn't go hungry."

"Oh!" A small cry escaped Mrs. Woodcutter's lips.

Charming turned to her and placed an armored hand gently on her shoulder.

"Upon questioning the family, I asked if anything else was missing," he said. "I didn't think to ask if anything new had turned up."

Mrs. Woodcutter nodded and lowered her head. "I found the slab of gingerbread in the cupboard just before you rode up. I couldn't tell anyone. How would it look? The woodcutter had just lost his job, and the both of us just lost the children." She wiped away a tear. "My dear sweet babies must have brought the gingerbread from the forest before they disappeared."

"That explains the trail of crumbs," said Stiltskin.

"And the smear of frosting on the bridge rail," said the witch.

Ulff's eyes grew wide. "The *children* left the frosting, not the troll."

"On their way to the castle," I whispered to Charming. "To take the letter to the king."

"Hansel and Gretel purloined the letter," he said, "and set off for the castle. They thought to convince Your Majesty to change his mind. But those poor children, hungry and cold, stomachs no doubt grumbling, must have been tempted by the sweet aromas herein and slipped into this very pantry." He patted the pantry door.

Ulff nodded wisely. "To swipe more food. Hey! That explains the scratching sounds." He turned to Sir Roderick. "And you locked them in!"

"A complete misunderstanding, I assure you," said Sir Roderick. "Cook said they were squirrels."

"I said no such thing!" said Cook. "I only heard scratching. *You* said it was squirrels."

"Well, *one* of us did," said Sir Roderick.

"And now, without further ado, I give you"—Charming seized the pantry handle—"Hansel and Gretel." He pulled open the door.

The woodcutter's children sat sprawled on the pantry floor, surrounded by empty cake tins and half-eaten tarts. Jam streaked their faces. Chocolate smeared their clothes. They blinked in the sudden light, and Hansel let out a small burp.

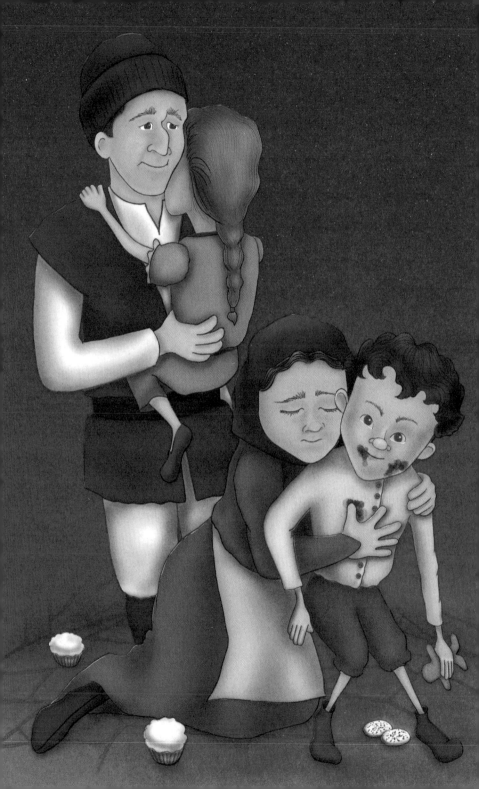

29

A Weasel of a Knave

My babies!" cried Mrs. Woodcutter.

"Huzzah!" cheered the court.

"Well done!" The king clapped the prince on the shoulder.

Then he caught my eye.

"Thank you," he told me in a low voice.

He turned to the crowd.

"Effective immediately, the royal woodcutter's job is officially restored," he decreed. "As is the royal dung farmer's."

"Huzzah!" cried the court again.

The Woodcutters gathered the children in their arms.

The king's men began unchaining the troll.

Sir Roderick rubbed his hands together. "All's well that ends well, then. Squirrels are not infesting the royal pantry. The children have been found, safe and sound and well fed. They can scamper off home with their parents and live happily ever after. No harm, no foul, as they say."

Ulff elbowed me. "Something doesn't smell right with that one," he murmured. "He had something to do with this. I *know* he did."

"He does want to be heir to the throne," I said. "What better way than to make Charming look like a bungling muttonhead?"

Ulff glared at Sir Roderick. His bristly red face grew redder. And bristlier.

"That lowdown, scurvy-ridden weasel of a knave," he said. "Besmirching someone as fine as the prince."

He turned to me. "So what did he do exactly?"

I chewed my lip. "Well," I said. "I can't prove it, but everything started to happen after the king put the prince in charge of the castle. Suddenly the woodcutter is secretly fired and the castle grows bone cold."

"Making the prince look bad." Ulff's eyes grew wide. "And Roderick's the jackanapes what wrote the letter! *And* sealed it with the ring he stole from the king."

"And lost it down the dung chute when he tried to put it back," I said.

Ulff shook his head. "And those wee sweet Woodcutter children. Brought the letter to the castle, thinking to beg the king for their father's job back, only to find themselves locked in the pantry."

I nodded. "I think that was a bit of luck Roderick wasn't counting on. Cook alerted him to the scratching before Hansel and Gretel could get to the king. Roderick took the letter, locked them in, claimed they were squirrels—"

"And blamed the whole thing on the prince." Ulff shook his head again. "*Then* let the king send the prince off on a wild-goose chase, searching the kingdom for them."

"And me with him," I said. "I think Sir Roderick recognized me, when no one else in the palace did. I think he had already planned to fire my father, and he saw in me the opportunity to. He knew I'd be found out eventually—he'd make sure of it. What better excuse to get rid of the dung farmer?"

"And stink up the castle, what with all that dung going unfarmed." Ulff shook his head. "A cold, smelly castle, and our fine prince taking all the blame for it."

"Yes." I sighed. "But we have no evidence. There's no proof Sir Roderick did any of it."

Ulff frowned. "So he just gets away with it?"

"For now," I said. "We'll need to keep a close eye on him."

Ulff nodded. "No telling what the scoundrel might try next."

I pulled Ulff to the side as lords and ladies jostled from the kitchen. The Woodcutters followed, Mrs. Woodcutter carrying Hansel while Gretel rode on her father's shoulders. The witch came next, then the king's men and the troll. As he passed by, the troll turned his enormous eyes on me and gave a shaggy nod.

Mr. Stiltskin sidled after them, and I spotted the edge of a small mitten poking out from one of his pockets. Ulff spotted it, too. He stepped in front of the peddler, drew himself up to his full height, pinned Stiltskin with a glower worthy of the most fearsome of the fiercest king's men, and held out his hand.

Stiltskin stopped short. He opened his mouth. Then he looked at Ulff, sighed, and handed over the mitten without a word. As he darted away, he swiped a soup ladle from the cook's worktable and stashed it in his coat.

Ulff held up the mitten. "He *was* following us through the woods. Thinking to snatch up whatever whatnots the prince dropped, and scaring us near out of our boots. But at least we got our luck back." He frowned at the mitten. "Though I think we did better with it missing."

He tucked the mitten in his hat.

I glanced at Sir Roderick, who had mingled with the lords and ladies crowding their way out the door.

I wasn't the only one looking.

The king quietly watched Sir Roderick slink away from the kitchens. He rubbed his chin in thought.

"You know, we may not be alone in keeping an eye on him," I told Ulff.

30

An Assistant to the Prince

lunk.

Clank.

"Hunf."

Ulff and I hoisted Charming onto Darnell.

"To the cottage!" The prince spurred his faithful

steed to a trot, and we set off.

It was midnight. The castle towered above us. The

stench of the dung pit rose through the dark. My father's

voice thundered through the air.

"Lout!" he boomed. "Quit your snoring. I'll not have you wake the king."

"Snout!" he bawled. "Chew with your mouth shut. The king won't put up with crumbs on his cart path, and neither will I."

"Gerald!" he barked. "Put your back into it. That dung won't crank itself."

For that's what they were doing: cranking dung.

My father had built a dung-scooping contraption on the back of the cart. It looked suspiciously like the one from my drawing, but I wasn't brave or foolish enough to point that out to him.

Now Gerald cranked. My father bellowed. Lout and Snout ate sandwiches and napped under the cart.

As we passed, my father gave me a nod. He tried to hide it, but I think I saw his chest puff up ever so slightly.

In recent days, he'd been going about the village telling everyone he came across, "Dung farming was good enough for my father and my father's father and his father before him. But my boy Nobbin, he's smart. Too smart for the dung pit, that one. He's living up at the castle now. The king can't hardly run the kingdom without him."

My own chest puffed up at the thought of it.

The king could run things just fine, but I *was* living in the castle now. That made me proud. But it wasn't what puffed my chest.

What puffed my chest were two words: *my boy.* My father called me *my boy.*

"So." Ulff rubbed a crust of sleep from his eye. "What is it that has us setting out at this time of night?"

"It seems," said Charming, "we have another food thief in our midst."

Ulff perked up. "At the witch's place?"

"One would think." The prince frowned. "But no, this robber wasn't after gingerbread. This one stole porridge."

"Porridge?" Ulff gave a shudder.

"From the bears' cottage," said Charming.

"Bears?" Ulff shook his head. "There must be easier places to pilfer porridge from."

"If this crime wave keeps up," said the prince, "we'll need to ask the village scribe to letter us some business cards." He held out a hand, tracing in the air the words he imagined in his head. "Prince Charming, Royal Detective."

Ulff held out his own hand. "With His Faithful Guard, Ulff, and Noble Assistant, Nobbin."

"Swill," I said. "Make sure they say Nobbin Swill."

Author's Note
History Was a Stinky Place

Crumbled! is a work of fiction. The characters (including those plucked from fairy tales) are made up, as are the setting and the plot. You may be thinking I made up the garderobe, the dung pit, and the whole dung farming operation, too, just to make Nobbin's life miserable.

Nope.

In the days before indoor plumbing, these things were very real. People had to do their business somewhere. Ordinary folks used chamber pots or buckets. Royal folks used chamber pots, too. But they also had garderobes.

Garderobes were closet-sized chambers built into the outer wall of the castle, often jutting out from the side of the castle itself. Inside was the toilet—a stone bench, often fitted with a wooden seat with a hole in it.

The hole led to a chute that ran down through the stone and emptied into a moat, stream, or pit below. Very important people in the castle, such as the king, had personal, one-hole garderobes. Less important people used garderobes that sported several holes, sort of like public restrooms today, but without today's restroom stalls to keep the private stuff private.

Garderobes usually had small windows cut into the stone. The windows let in light and air and made garderobes bitterly cold in the winter. They were also meant to let out the stench, but there was a lot of stench, and most of it did not get out. Luckily, people back then thought the smelly fumes would ward off fleas and moths. They began hanging their clothes in their garderobes to safeguard them from crawly creatures. A garderobe, then, became a place to actually guard robes. The word *garderobe*, in turn, became our modern word *wardrobe*.

What goes into the dung pit must eventually come

out, and that job fell to the dung farmer. Dung farmers were also called gong farmers because the stuff they shoveled was often called gong.

Dung farming—or gong farming—has been called one of the worst jobs in history. Dung farmers had to climb down into the pit, shovel the dung—or gong— out, and cart it away, often to be spread as fertilizer on fields of crops. It was filthy, smelly, unhealthy, often hazardous work. Dung farmers developed diseases. Sometimes, overcome by the fumes, they passed out in the pit. The stench may not have warded off fleas, but it could fell a full-grown dung farmer.

Nobody wanted to smell a cart full of dung rolling down the road, so dung farmers had to carry out their work at night, when people weren't awake to notice the stink. Because of this, dung farmers were sometimes known as night men, the dung they shoveled known as night soil. Dung farmers themselves stank as bad as their work, so they weren't allowed to live in town. They and their stink had to live on the outskirts, where they wouldn't offend less smelly residents.

Dung farmers were paid well, often many times more than common laborers. They also made money from the things they found. Garderobe users sometimes lost things, such as coins or jewelry, down the dung chute. Other times, people chucked unwanted items into the chute, using it as a sort of trash dump. Dung farmers fished these things from the muck and sold them.

So no, I didn't make up garderobes, dung pits, and dung farming. They are all true. But yes, I did put them in the story to make Nobbin miserable!